HOW TO SELL YOUR FAMILY TO THE ALIENS

HOW TO SELL YOUR FAMILY TO THE ALIENS

PAUL NOTH

BLOOMSBURY

NEW YORK LONDON OXFORD NEW DELHI SYDNEY

First published in the United States of America in April 2018
by Bloomsbury Children's Books
www.bloomsbury.com

Bloomsbury is a registered trademark of Bloomsbury Publishing Plc

For information about permission to reproduce selections from this book, write to
Permissions, Bloomsbury Children's Books, 1385 Broadway, New York, New York 10018
Bloomsbury books may be purchased for business or promotional use. For information on bulk
purchases please contact Macmillan Corporate and Premium Sales Department at
specialmarkets@macmillan.com

Library of Congress Cataloging-in-Publication Data
Names: Noth, Paul, author.
Title: How to sell your family to the aliens / by Paul Noth.
Description: New York : Bloomsbury, 2018.
Summary: Ten-year-old Hap's grandmother has experimented on his family and confined them
to the basement of a mansion paid for by his father's inventions, but his plan to sell her to
aliens goes awry.
Identifiers: LCCN 2017024253 (print) • LCCN 2017038526 (e-book)
ISBN 978-1-68119-657-2 (hardcover) • ISBN 978-1-68119-658-9 (e-book)
Subjects: | CYAC: Family life—Fiction. | Grandmothers—Fiction. | Ability—Fiction. |
Inventors—Fiction. | Extraterrestrial beings—Fiction. | Humorous stories.
Classification: LCC PZ7.1.N66 How 2018 (print) | LCC PZ7.1.N66 (e-book) |
DDC [Fic]—dc23
LC record available at https://lccn.loc.gov/2017024253

Book design by Kimi Weart
Typeset by Westchester Publishing Services
Printed and bound in the U.S.A. by Berryville Graphics Inc., Berryville, Virginia
2 4 6 8 10 9 7 5 3 1

FOR PARNELL

HOW TO SELL YOUR FAMILY TO THE ALIENS

FBI WARNING:

THIS BOOK CONTAINS INFORMATION—PARTICULARLY THE PARTS ABOUT SELLING YOUR FAMILY TO THE ALIENS—THAT MAY BE DANGEROUS. THE AUTHOR, HAPPY CONKLIN JUNIOR, INCLUDES THESE PASSAGES IN THE INTEREST OF THE GENERAL PUBLIC'S UNDERSTANDING, KNOWLEDGE, AND BETTERMENT. THE AUTHOR NEITHER CONDONES NOR ENCOURAGES THE USE OF THIS INFORMATION FOR THE PURPOSE OF READERS SELLING THEIR OWN FAMILIES TO THE ALIENS.

CONTINUE READING AT YOUR OWN RISK.

A note from Happy Conklin Junior:

The lawyers say I can't write this book unless I start with that FBI-approved warning. As you may know, my family has had a long history of trouble with the FBI, but I would like to state publicly that I have no hard feelings toward that fine organization or its agents. After all, they were only doing their job.

Sincerely,

Happy Conklin Jr.

PART 1

WHY TO SELL YOUR FAMILY TO THE ALIENS

GRANDMA

CHAPTER 1

MY FAMILY

Before you assume I'm a bad person, you should know that I had originally only planned on selling Grandma to the aliens. Not my whole family. And I would not have sold her without excellent reasons.

First of all, I wanted money. Second of all, I had a grandma.

When I say "Grandma" I hope you're not picturing some sweet old lady who baked me cookies every day. My grandma only baked cookies once a week, and even then they weren't for me but for my dad. And actually she didn't bake them herself either—her personal chef did. My dad's inventions paid for her to have a chef, three maids, a butler, a bunch of security guards, a chauffeur, and a footman, who I guess did something to her feet. I don't want to know what.

Dad's whole purpose in life was to please Grandma. He did all the work, and she got all the money. So she had the five floors of our house all to herself, while Mom, Dad, my five sisters, and I shared two rooms in the basement.

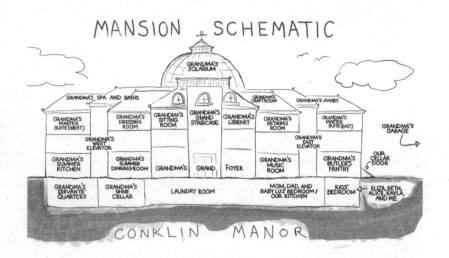

Grandma's security guards kept us kids out of her fancy part of the house, where there were chandeliers and windows and stuff. We weren't allowed to use her elevator. We weren't allowed to use the servants' elevator. If Grandma saw me even reading the sign on the servants' elevator, she'd throw open her window and scream, "Don't *you* read that sign! That sign is for my servants!" and slam it shut.

But even though I was poor, I didn't get any of that good poor-kid stuff, like people feeling sorry for you.

Everyone assumed I was rich when they heard my name was Happy Conklin Junior.

"Your father's *the* Hap Conklin?" they'd say, smiling as they remembered how famous Dad is, then frowning as they remembered how annoying he is.

The thought of my dad is probably making you frown too. I already know what you think of him, so you don't have to tell me how much you hate his TV infomercials, radio fomercials, and Internet fomercials. I know you're tired of his loud billboard fomercials, his bus fomercials, his blimp fomercials, and his tree fomercials. I get it. You just want to walk past a tree in peace, or have a little silence as you board a bus or a blimp, without him screaming down at you: "I'm Hap Conklin!" I know how those words have come to feel like a dental drill going into your eye. I know.

But remember, he actually invented all that stuff in those fomercials. He worked really hard on his inventions, and no one can say that they haven't changed the world. Especially his bestseller:

Until Buns of Abs came along, people didn't even know that they *wanted* ab-shaped

muscles on their buns, let alone that it was achievable through diet, exercise, and corrective pants.

Of course, not all his creations have been so successful.

That's One Handsome Baby, like most of Dad's inventions, started out as Grandma's idea for the next big money-making wonder product.

Babies annoyed her. "Too unpredictable," she always said. She especially hated not being able to tell boy babies from girl babies. So Dad invented a topical cream to make boy babies grow beards. It worked instantly: a newborn grew facial hair faster than a lumberjack werewolf. Fortunately, Grandma only ever tested that product on one baby. Unfortunately, that baby's name was Happy Conklin Junior. I have had to shave three times a day, every day, ever since I could hold a razor.

But of course, no one bought That's One Handsome Baby. The public did not share Grandma's feelings about baby gender

appearance. Also, infants are terrible at shaving.

Most of us Conklin kids had one invention or another tested on us. I'm luckier than some of my sisters. Next to them, being a ten-year-old

boy with a beard wasn't so bad. Take my younger sister Kayla, for example.

Grandma still didn't like unpredictable babies, bearded or not. So next she tested Hap Conklin's Baby Master— a product that proved to be highly defective—on baby Kayla.

Nine years later, Kayla still wears a yellow headband every day and talks to an imaginary honeybee named Alphonso.

In short, my life couldn't get any worse—or so I thought, until our mom had to go out of town for a few weeks.

A little background on Mom:

She was from a country called Moldova in Eastern Europe. Fifteen years ago, she came to the United States on a work visa to be a laundress at Conklin Manor. Mom didn't speak any English, a fact that did not prevent her and Dad from falling in love. They had to hide the relationship from Grandma, who would not have approved.

But then Mom became, as they say, "with child," and Grandma figured out what had been going on. Boy, was she furious! She had far grander things in mind for her genius son than a rushed marriage to a Moldovan laundress. So Grandma threw Dad out of the house. He moved into Mom's servants' quarters down here in the basement.

Eventually, Grandma agreed to let them remain a couple, but only if they both signed a bunch of legal documents giving Grandma the power to nullify their union and deport Mom whenever she felt like it. Since then, I think Grandma has regarded our family as a growing but manageable pest problem in the basement.

Now, after fifteen years, Grandma was finally giving Mom a promotion from laundress to Director of Laundry. But first Mom had to complete some sort of advanced laundry training program at a hospitality school in Nevada.

With Mom gone, our lives went off a cliff.

Dad could not manage the simplest household task. Most of us kids began acting out in our worst behavior. Morale was in the toilet, and the toilet wouldn't flush.

Then came the horrible incident of my sister Alice and Squeep! the lizard.

CHAPTER 2

SQUEEP!

It will come as no surprise that "Beard Boy" has never been the most popular kid at school. Grandma forbade us any contact with TVs, video games, the Internet—all the favorite topics at my school—so I always had trouble finding normal things to talk about with my classmates. The only *other* things kids wanted to talk about were my beard and my famous family of freaks. I endured years of constant teasing, and by fifth grade I felt sure that school could not possibly get any worse for me.

But then I lost Squeep!, my class's pet lizard.

Maybe "lost" isn't the right word. Everyone in my grade had to take Squeep! home overnight to help us learn personal responsibility. I knew the risks of bringing that cute little lizard into the same bedroom as my sister Alice—especially with Mom away. Alice had been at her

SQUEEP! THE LIZARD... LOVED BY EVERYONE

9" 9"

very worst lately. I begged Ms. Jensen to excuse me from the assignment, but she insisted. All night long, I sat awake on my cot, holding Squeep! in both hands to protect him from Alice. But then, sometime close to morning, I accidentally fell asleep.

ALICE STEALS EVERYTHING ...

... AND THEN DENIES IT.

WHAT WOULD I WANT WITH A SLIMY OLD LIZARD, ANYWAY?!!

One of Grandma's experiments had left Alice with an ability to steal things and hide them away forever. Tattling on her was useless. Alice would deny everything and never be caught with any evidence. Also, if I had told Ms. Jensen the truth about Alice stealing Squeep!, the police might have become involved. My family was already under investigation by the FBI, for reasons I'll soon explain. I *couldn't* betray my own family like that. So instead, I told my class that Squeep! had run away.

The whole school had loved Squeep! (aka "Squeepers," aka "Sir Squeepsalot," aka "Squeep City, USA"). When I lost him, I lost every ally I ever had at that place—kids *and* adults. A week later, this boy named Happy still walked home every day in tears. Until, wiping my eyes one Friday afternoon, I chanced upon the one thing I wanted most in the world, the one thing I knew could transform me from an isolated oddball into a regular kid:

A TV!

It sat out on a curb with a neighbor's garbage bins. I stared down at it in disbelief. I felt like a genie had granted my greatest wish.

My parents fully supported Grandma's ban on television, because they weren't exactly normal people either. But with Mom away, it felt like all the rules were out the window. Everyone else was getting away with murder, why shouldn't I?

It never even occurred to me that the TV might be broken. Fate could not be that cruel.

I could barely lift that boxy, old-fashioned TV off the grass. Yet somehow I carried it the whole two blocks to Conklin Grounds. I lugged it through the servants' gate, keeping an eye out for Grandma's security guards, all the way to our door, and  then down the stairs to the two little basement rooms where my family lived.

If Mom had been home, she would have caught me with it before I had even reached the last step. But I only had to worry about Dad, and I could probably have driven a whole truckload of TVs straight through our kitchen without him noticing.

I peeked around the corner into what was both the kitchen and our parents' bedroom. Dad stood by the stove. He held his newest invention, a braided ring of golden wires, in one hand while absently stirring a pot of beans with the other. An enormous plastic ketchup bottle stood at the ready beside the pot. With Mom away, Dad had been "cooking" for us.

He always squirted a lot of ketchup into our nightly

dinner of beans. At breakfast, he sprinkled a little sugar on our breakfast beans. But lunch was the best. Just plain beans.

Well, it wasn't so great on school days, when the bean juice soaked through the bottom of my paper lunch bag before I even got to homeroom. Then the other kids would usually steal the bag from me, smash it over my face, and yell, "Beard of beans! Beard Boy's got a beard of beans!" Then they would all do the Make-Beard-Boy-Cry Dance. I didn't like this dance, because it made me cry, but I had to admit that over the years some of the kids had gotten pretty good at it. Although in terms of rhythm, style, and flair, none of them could match Ms. Dalton, the principal. When she jumped into the Make-Beard-Boy-Cry Dance all the kids and teachers would dance back into a half circle to watch her amazing moves. You could really see why she was principal.

But that's all in the past now, I thought, admiring my new TV. I would finally be able to talk to my classmates like a normal kid, and say normal-kid things like, "Yeah, I saw that show too," without it being a bald-faced lie, or a stubbly-faced lie. Heaving the TV aloft, I tiptoed silent as a ninja into the kitchen. Suddenly, I heard a voice singing in Romanian. Had Mom come home?

But it was only Kayla, singing one of Mom's Moldovan folk songs to our youngest sister, Baby Lu. Mom had set up a "Safety Schedule" so that one of us would always be watching Baby Lu during her absence. Kayla looked up and shook her yellow-banded head at the ridiculous sight of me lugging the enormous TV through the kitchen. But Baby Lu grinned and said my name, which she pronounced "Bapy." Her eyes brightened, and she gave me such a big gummy smile that I had to smile back. "You can do it, Bapy," her smile seemed to say. "You got this, big brother."

Deeply encouraged, I carried the TV into the bedroom I shared with my five sisters. Here, I made a Sister Schematic, so you don't get too confused:

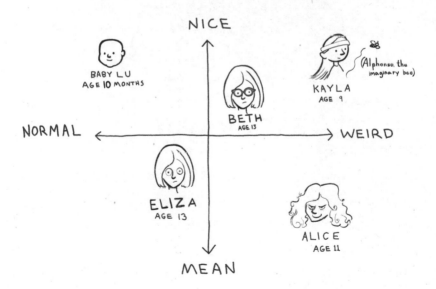

SISTER SCHEMATIC

NICE

BABY LU
AGE 10 MONTHS

KAYLA
AGE 9

(Alphonso, the imaginary bee)

BETH
AGE 13

NORMAL ← → WEIRD

ELIZA
AGE 13

ALICE
AGE 11

MEAN

See how there's a Weirdness Axis and a Meanness Axis? Well, you can blame Grandma's experiments for all of the weirdness, and probably a fair amount of the meanness too. But please don't blame my parents. Granted, Dad is pretty out-to-lunch about most things. And Mom? I don't think she realized how dangerous the experiments could be until what happened to Baby Kayla, nine years ago. After that, Mom stopped allowing Grandma access to any of her babies, which finally put a stop to the experiments.

BABY KAYLA

CHAPTER 3

THE TWINS

As I lugged my new TV into our bedroom, I worried about how my three older sisters might react. Luckily, they were too distracted to notice.

As usual, the twins were screaming at Alice. Beth had her glasses off, so I couldn't tell her apart from Eliza.

"You little thief!" screamed one twin. "Where's my sweatshirt?"

"You steal everything!" screamed the other.

You wouldn't be able to tell them apart either. Unlike so-called identical twins, Beth and Eliza were *actually identical*—physically and vocally indistinguishable from each other. The only thing that allowed anyone to tell them apart were those green-framed specs. The moment Beth removed the glasses, NOBODY—no parent, sibling, teacher, or facial recognition software—could tell Eliza from Beth or Beth from Eliza. In photos and mirrors, they couldn't even tell themselves apart.

Ironically, the green-framed glasses that prevented their identicalness also caused it.

See, back when the twins were babies, Grandma had desperately wanted another blockbuster self-improvement product to build on the success of Buns of Abs. This new product wouldn't just give you amazing abs on your buns, it would give you whatever kind of body you wanted. As usual, Dad rose to the challenge and created Hap Conklin's Perfect-O-Specs.

HAP CONKLIN'S PERFECT-O-SPECS

step 1:

The Specs were the first product Grandma ever tested on her grandchildren. It happened years before I was born, and nobody ever talked about it— the details of Grandma's experiments were considered a dangerous topic in my family. But I had always assumed

step 2:

step 3:

that Beth and Eliza had been born fraternal twins, and Grandma had used the Specs to make them identical. Beth, as you will see, had different theories.

However it happened, the experiment was deemed a great success. The Specs worked amazingly well, and they would have been an enormous commercial hit if the US government hadn't banned them before the product launch. The feds claimed that glasses which allowed people to steal each other's physical appearance would lead to a giant identity theft crime wave. This marked the beginning of my family's troubles with the FBI.

In order to stay identical to Eliza, several times a day Beth would stare at Eliza through the Specs and flick them on. If Beth neglected to do this, by the end of the day her skin would begin to freckle. She hated those freckles, probably because they reminded everyone of Alice. She never let a day go by without making sure she looked just like Eliza, because after the freckling process had started, who knows what other changes might follow? She didn't really know who, or what, she might turn into.

For good reason, Beth guarded and protected the Specs as though her life depended on it. As far as we knew, they were the last pair on the planet. But she never wore them in public, for fear that she would suddenly be surrounded by men in dark suits and FBI windbreakers who would try to take her glasses away.

CHAPTER 4

MY TV

So there I was, lugging the TV into our bedroom, while the twins screamed at Alice.

"You criminal!" screamed one twin. "Where are my corduroys?"

"You steal everything!" screamed the other.

"Ha!" said Alice, denying it as usual. "What would I want with your disgusting corduroys?"

"You stole my strawberry shampoo!" screamed a twin.

"Ha!" said Alice. "As though I would ever even dream of *touching* your cheap pathetic shampoo!"

"I need my own room!" howled a twin. Actually, I knew this was Eliza, because Eliza howled "I need my own room!" about twenty thousand times a day.

I lowered the TV onto my cot. My sweaty arms shook with exertion, or maybe excitement. My own TV. I actually had one! I could finally start living like a normal human being.

The cord reached the nearest baseboard outlet. I plugged it in and sat down in front of the screen. After a long, deep breath, I turned the power button slowly.

It went *click*. Then nothing. I tried it again. *Click* off. *Click* on. Still nothing. *Click-click, click-click, click-click*. Nothing, nothing, nothing. *Stay calm*, I told myself. *Don't panic*.

But a moment later I was flicking every switch madly, turning every knob, spinning every dial in a flurry of frustration, and then I was banging both hands hard atop that lifeless old box like an angry gorilla. *Bang! Bang! Bang! Bang! Bang!*

I realized the whole room had gone quiet.

Alice and the twins stood in front of my cot. When I looked up at them, their silent giggles became howling screams of laughter.

"You actually thought that piece of junk would work!" shrieked Alice.

"Look at how sweaty he got carrying it!" screamed a twin.

"He probably gave himself ten hernias!" screamed the other.

"Look at his little face!"

"Aw, is someone gonna cry?"

Some evil jerk from my school had taught my big

sisters the Make-Beard-Boy-Cry Dance. As they began to sway and sing in unison, I clenched my jaw, tightened my fists, and fought to hold back the inevitable eruption of misery.

"Beard Boy's gonna c—"

But before the tears could arrive, Alice and the twins stopped singing. They looked over at our sister Kayla, who now approached with purposeful concentration. When Kayla moved like this, we all usually shut up to see what was about to happen. (Kayla, as you might remember from my helpful Sister Schematic, was at the farthest end of the Weirdness Axis.)

Striding up to the edge of my cot, Kayla scratched her yellow headband and stared down at the TV. While she examined it, her face formed the quick little expressions she made whenever she was talking to Alphonso, her imaginary bee.

Then her features calmed. Her arm moved fast. Her hand, with surgical precision, clamped on to the cord's connection into the back of the TV and made three clockwise turns.

An electric *pop*. A rising hum. A bloom of colored light.

"Thanks, Kayla," I whispered as the TV awoke like a sleeping angel.

HE'S NOT IMAGINARY.

27

She nodded and walked away.

"Know-it-all," said Alice.

"Traitor!" said Eliza. Or maybe Beth. No, probably Eliza.

But I didn't care because . . . I was actually watching TV! I knew this theme music from kids humming it on the playground. I had heard them imitate this deep-voiced announcer. This wasn't just any show, but the most popular show at my school: *Wrastlinsanity*! Actually, "popular" doesn't come close to describing the phenomenon of this program. If my school had been a religion, *Wrastlinsanity* would have been God.

The moment tasted sweeter than any cookie baked by Grandma's chef. Just seeing the names on the championship bracket, a list of playground legends, I felt bliss uninterrupted . . .

Until I noticed Alice. She lay back on her cot, secretly watching me from behind her little silver makeup compact. I clutched the TV protectively. I thought that if I kept both hands and both eyes on the set, maybe Alice wouldn't be able to steal it. Maybe.

How good a thief was Alice?

Once, during one of the government's investigations of our family, I watched her steal the handcuffs off the belt of an FBI agent without him noticing. Afterward, she showed me the contact lenses she had stolen from his eyes.

I would have bet everything I owned that she was the greatest thief of all time, only Alice had already stolen everything I owned. She had slipped Squeep! the lizard out of my hands the *instant* I fell asleep. She had swiped every crime novel I ever brought home, until the library revoked my card and started treating *me* like a criminal.

Where did she hide all the loot? Nobody knew, but my money was on that little silver makeup compact of hers. She was so stealthy and secretive that I had never even managed to learn the name of the invention Grandma had tested on her, which had surely caused these abilities. All I knew for certain was that once Alice stole something, you could forget about ever seeing it again. What Alice took stayed took for good.

But not this time! I thought, looking up boldly to meet the eyes peeking over her silver makeup compact. She flinched at the fierce look on my face. "Not this time, Alice," I whispered. This time I would be faster. This time I would be smarter.

This time, I swore, there was no way on heaven or earth that Alice was going to get my TV.

ALICE: ALWAYS LOOKING AT MAKEUP COMPACT, NEVER WEARS MAKEUP (VERY SUSPICIOUS).

CHAPTER 5

ALICE STEALS MY TV

Wrastlinsanity turned out to be as great as everybody said it was. By some unusual stroke of luck, I had tuned in to what would become one of the most famous matches in history. I got to watch the champ himself wrestle— Florida Pete, the world's strongest man. A seven-foot tower of bulging muscles.

Watching him in motion, I couldn't help but wish for my own pair of Perfect-O-Specs so that, if I ever saw him in person, I could make myself the twin of Florida Pete. All my life I had heard kids try to imitate his famous "gator whoop." But when Pete himself did it, the hairs on my neck stood up. I could see why the whoop alone scared some opponents straight out of the ring.

"And the chaaallenger!" said the deep-voiced announcer. "The Masked Flamenco!"

Two feet shorter than Florida Pete and thin as a rail, the Masked Flamenco wore a fancy spangled black jumpsuit and a black head mask embroidered with glittery red roses.

Well this shouldn't take long, I thought.

The bell dinged. Florida Pete charged. And the Masked Flamenco started *dancing*, as though to Spanish guitar music nobody else could hear. Rhythmically gyrating narrow hips, the Masked Flamenco traced intricate patterns in the air with long and gracefully snapping fingers. Familiar fingers.

Florida Pete swung five fast hammer-blows. Dancing around each, the Masked Flamenco slapped a forehand and then a backhand across Pete's face. *Slap-slap.* The crowd gasped. So did I. So did Pete. Then he whooped ferociously and leapt like a tiger.

As the Masked Flamenco tried to twirl away, only inches ahead of Pete's clawing grasps, it seemed we were all about to witness a brutal murder. I thought I might die of excitement, when the bell dinged to end the round.

"I'm Hap Conklin!" yelled a familiar voice.

It took me a moment to realize Dad was on the TV and not in our room. Conklin Industries turned out to be the main sponsor of *Wrastlinsanity.* This fomercial had Dad selling the new line of family-sized frozen dinners, including Hap Conklin's Chinese Cheesy Melt and Hap Conklin's Clockos, "The only frozen taco that tells the time."

Finally a break. I had needed to go to the bathroom since before leaving school. I unplugged the set. I'd have to take it with me, since I couldn't leave it alone with Alice.

But my arms had grown so stiff and sore that I could barely move them. I wedged my fingers under the TV and had to lean back with all my weight to hoist it up. Just keeping my balance hurt. The first step was excruciating. The second made me want to cry, as I realized that this would be my life from now on. If I ever left the TV, I would lose it. I could never go to sleep. I would have to carry it to school on Monday and take it around to all my classes. Overcome with pain and despair, I wanted to give up, to drop it on the floor, to break it and be done.

But then I thought of Florida Pete. He hadn't become the world's strongest man by giving up. *Yes, this is hard,* I told myself. *Yes, the next couple months will be even harder. But think of how strong you're going to become. Think of Florida Pete. Florida Pete.*

Just repeating the name made me feel stronger, and I carried that TV straight out of the bedroom and into the hallway. Now I wondered how I ever could have thought of dropping this wonderful machine, my ticket to normalcy, to acceptance at school and to escape from my family at home. I carried it faster so as not to miss anything after the commercial.

Halfway to the bathroom, I heard something tiny approaching, below and in front of me. A *ticky-ticky* skittering sound. I looked down in time to see a little green animal scurrying past my shoe. I knew that exclamation-point-like shape. I knew those brown spots, that adorable little tail.

"Squeep!" I said.

It was he. Any doubt about his identity vanished when he turned and looked back at the sound of his name. Then he darted away.

"No, wait!" I yelled, setting down the TV.

I dove after him, through the air. I felt his scaly skin zip between my fingers as I landed. Then he vanished under the closet door, leaving behind a strong scent of strawberry shampoo.

Oh no, I thought.

Rolling over, I looked back down the hall. The TV was gone.

Deep down, I already knew what had happened, but I wouldn't admit it to myself until I had searched through the whole closet for Squeep! and paced back and forth and down the hallway over and over looking for the TV. Gone and gone.

Alice had gotten me good. A classic lizard diversion. I walked back into the bedroom and stared down at her. Leaning back on her cot, she looked into her silver makeup compact with the smallest possible smile on her freckly face. Where was she hiding it all? I kept thinking. Her nightstand was bare, except for her round hairbrush—which Alice cleaned so seldom that it had come to resemble a small, red Persian cat.

The makeup compact! She had to be hiding it all in that little silver compact! But how? How could she hide so much inside something so small?

"No!" said one of the twins. "She stole it already?"

Beth, now wearing her glasses, walked up beside me and stared down at Alice.

"Ha!" said Alice. "You think I'd actually *want* that ridiculous old TV?"

"Unbelievable," said Beth. "What's the matter with you, Alice? You crazy kleptomaniac."

Alice, who hated being called a kleptomaniac, struck back with the word that would hurt Beth the most.

"Phony!" yelled Alice. "Four-eyed phony!"

Beth's face flushed. She threw a hard slap at Alice, but the latter was quicker than anyone and easily dodged it.

"You'll pay for trying to hit me," said Alice. "You'll pay big-time!"

"I need my own room!" screamed Eliza.

As I turned away and walked toward the bathroom, I thought, *I can't take any more of this! I cannot take one more day of these people. I need to do something. Something big! Something PERMANENT!*

THIS IS NOT WHAT THE ALIENS LOOK LIKE. I JUST DREW THIS TO FOOL PEOPLE WHO ARE FLIPPING AHEAD IN THE BOOK TO FIND OUT WHAT THE ALIENS LOOK LIKE.

CHAPTER 6

I STOP SHAVING

I didn't shave that night or the next morning. Why bother? I thought. Let them tease me. Let them sing their mocking songs and dance their evil dances. I didn't care anymore! Now I only cared about getting back what was mine. The TV. The lizard. Everything. But so far, I didn't have a plan . . . except to lie in bed and let my face turn into a giant tumbleweed.

On Saturdays my sisters all slept a little later. Eliza rose first and headed to the bathroom to shower. As eldest sibling, she got the first turn. A moment later Beth and Alice got into another screaming match. I tried to ignore it, until I realized what they were actually arguing about. Then I shot up in bed, unable to believe my ears.

"You stole them right off my dresser!" yelled Beth. "You stole my Specs!"

"HA!" yelled Alice. "Why on earth would I ever even touch your disgusting idiot glasses?"

As Alice stormed out of the room, I noticed that she had a pillowcase wrapped around her left wrist, for some unfathomable reason.

Could she really have stolen Beth's glasses? The Specs were like *part* of Beth. It would be like stealing someone's name, or their age, or their history. I looked to Kayla to see what she made of all this, but she was still snoozing. In my family, you learned to sleep through anything.

Beth slumped down onto her bare cot. She looked hard at the back of her hands as though waiting for the freckles to appear.

"She really stole your Specs?" I said, walking toward her.

"While I was sleeping," said Beth. Now I saw the tears shining down her face. As much as my sisters drove me crazy, I hated to see them cry. I tried to say the most comforting thing I could think of.

"There, there," I said.

Of course, this didn't help. So I tried, "It's going to be okay."

"No it's not!" said Beth. "I'm going to *change* into . . . I don't even know who! I can feel it happening already."

"Well, so what if you don't look *exactly* like Eliza?" I said. "It's not like you guys are that pretty anyway."

Boy, comforting people was a lot harder than it looked.

"It's more than just my appearance, Hap," she said. "I'm going to become a different person, understand? I don't remember *who I was* before the glasses. Maybe I was never even her twin."

"What? Of course you guys are twins. You just have freckles. Big deal."

"What if they aren't just freckles? What if I'm about to turn into a speckled little lab rat or something?"

"Don't be crazy," I said. "You can't possibly be a rat. Grandma's totally opposed to animal testing. She only experimented on her grandchildren."

But Beth went on staring at her hands as though expecting them to shrink down into little rat claws at any moment. I tried to put myself in her shoes. How would I feel if tomorrow I wake up, look in the mirror, and see a complete stranger staring back at me? The thought was terrifying.

"We should team up, Beth," I said. "Against Alice. Let's get your Specs back, and my TV, and the lizard. Everything. If we work together, we can figure out"—I lowered my voice—"how she does it."

Beth glanced around nervously. I had broached a dangerous subject. How Alice did it, and the details of that experiment, were *big* secrets protected by both Alice and Grandma.

"Okay," Beth whispered, her eyes flashing with determination. "Let's do it. Tell me what you know, and I'll tell you what I know."

"I think Alice hides everything she steals in that little silver makeup compact of hers."

"Well, duh," whispered Beth. "Eliza and I figured that much out years ago. The question isn't where, it's how. What's the trick of it? How does she hide so much inside something so little?"

"To know that," I whispered, "I need to know what happened to Alice. What Grandma did to her. What product was she testing?"

"I don't know." Beth's voice dropped to near silence now. "But I do know where we can find out. Have you ever heard of the Black Room?"

"No," I said. "What black room?"

"It's where Grandma keeps all the secrets that she needs to hide from the FBI. Everything about Alice is in there."

"How do we get to the Bla—"

"That's enough!" said an angry voice.

We looked over and saw our sister Kayla striding toward us.

"You guys shouldn't even be talking about that room," she said. "It's too dangerous."

"Kayla!" I said. "You can help us."

"Yeah," said Beth. "You know everything, Kayla. Help me get my Specs back."

Kayla scratched at the yellow headband, which she had worn every day of her life since Grandma had tested the Baby Master on her.

The Baby Master's head-gear was designed to read your baby's thoughts and text her planned direction to your smartphone, thus allowing you to predict your toddler's toddlings. Or that's what it *would* have done, if some-

thing hadn't gone horribly wrong with Dad's prototype. Instead of a predictable baby, the world got Kayla, a baby who could predict things.

Now, at nine, Kayla knew the answer to almost any question I could think of. She certainly knew all of Alice's secrets, but she refused to share them with us, no matter how many times we begged her.

"Come on, Kayla," pleaded Beth. "Alice stole my Specs this time!"

"We're doing this," I said. "With or without you, Kayla."

"You guys don't understand," said Kayla, massaging the headband at her temple, "how dangerous it is to even be talking about the Black Room. Things will get *very bad*."

"How could they get any worse?" I said. "I'm missing everything on TV, and she's turning into a rat!"

"Beth, you're not a lab rat," said Kayla. "None of us are. At least not in the literal sense."

"Whose side are you on, anyway?" said Beth. "Do you realize what's happening here? Alice stole my Specs!"

"Alice *has* them, yes," said Kayla, looking past us. "But she didn't consciously steal them. She took the thing that took them."

"Don't defend her!" said Beth. "She's a thief!"

"Yeah," I said. "You should be helping the victims, not abetting the criminal."

"I know," said Kayla, nodding.

"So help us!" said Beth.

"I can't."

"Why not?" yelled Beth and I together.

"Because," said Kayla. "Alphonso."

At the mention of Alphonso, Beth threw her hands up and I clasped my head in despair.

"Not Alphonso again," said Beth.

"Everything's Alphonso with you, Kayla," I said. "Alphonso-Alphonso-Alphonso!"

At this point you might be wondering, what's the deal with Alphonso?

CHAPTER 7

ALPHONSO THE BEE

Alphonso was an imaginary honeybee that Kayla insisted was real. Here's how she explained it:

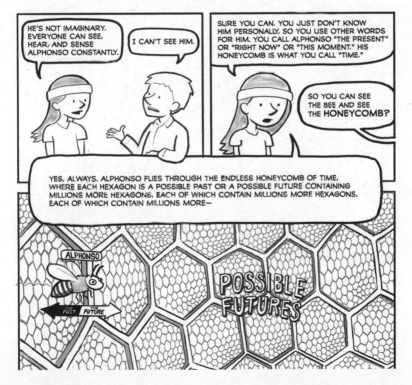

I didn't see how Alphonso could be. Or how he could be a bee. But I could not deny that Alphonso, imaginary or not, gave Kayla *real* information. I mean, top-quality intel about unknowables future and past. This could be great, like when she fixed my TV, or like when she predicted snow days so I could put off doing my homework, but it also gave her a tendency to rain on one's parade. And this morning she was coming down like a thunderstorm.

Beth sighed. "So, what's the stupid bee saying now?"

"That today is very dangerous," said Kayla. "You and Happy shouldn't even be talking about the Black Room. It will lead to disaster. You need to stop, and if you don't I will trap you and *make* you stop."

"But that's not fair," I said.

"Alice steals our stuff, and we're supposed to do nothing?" said Beth.

"I agree it's not fair," said Kayla, scratching her headband. "But at least give me until the end of breakfast to work out a solution with Alphonso."

"You have half an hour," said Beth, rising. "Then I'm going to the Black Room."

As Beth stormed out of the bedroom, Kayla turned to me.

"If either of you plans anything that dangerous today, you know I'll have to trap you."

"Why don't you trap Alice?" I said. "And make her give us our stuff back?"

"I'm working on that," said Kayla. "But that's only a small facet of the problem we're facing. I need to get Mom home. None of this would be happening if she were here."

"You got that right," I said. "What's taking her so long, anyway? How much can there possibly be to learn about laundry?"

"How much can there possibly be . . . ," repeated Kayla, in that absent way she had when talking to Alphonso. A moment later, her eyes popped open and her face flushed.

"Oh no!" she yelled. "Why didn't I see this before?"

She ran out of the bedroom, leaving me to wonder what that bee had told her now.

HERE'S ANOTHER EXAMPLE OF WHAT THE ALIENS DON'T LOOK LIKE FOR THOSE PEOPLE WHO KEEP FLIPPING AHEAD TO FIND OUT WHAT THE ALIENS LOOK LIKE.

CHAPTER 8

THE GREAT INVENTOR

Baby Lu smiled at me and reached up her arms for me to take her out of her playpen. How could I resist this from the cutest of all possible babies?

I lifted her up and carried her to the counter to fix her a bowl of breakfast beans. Eliza, freshly showered and in her purple sweater, stood near the stove. She reached out for the baby.

"Give her here," said Eliza. "Today's my day to watch her. It's on the Safety Schedule."

"I'm just going to feed her," I said. "Then you can take her."

"Whatever," said Eliza, shrugging.

Then she carried her own bowl into the bedroom to eat by herself. Whenever our room was empty, Eliza liked to go in there and sit alone. I assumed that in those moments she could pretend that she was an only child in a bedroom all her own where she could put up posters of horses on the walls without Alice stealing them the next minute.

As I sat Baby Lu on my lap to feed her, I noticed Kayla pacing around the table, in a deep silent conversation with Alphonso.

Beth sat staring daggers at Alice, who pretended not to notice.

Dad had clearly been up all night tinkering with his new invention. If Mom had been home, she might have convinced him to get some sleep. He was rushing to get the Golden Hoop assembled in time for his big weekly meeting with Grandma.

The thought of these Saturday meetings always made my mouth water, because that's where Grandma served her chef's amazing freshly baked cookies. Sometimes Dad would remember to pocket a few of those delicious masterpieces to bring home for me.

Baby Lu and I played the bean-face game: I would give her a bite of beans, and she would make the most disgusted face possible, which would crack me up. Then I would take a bite of beans, and pull an even *more* disgusted face, which would crack her up. Baby Lu had invented this game herself. She had an amazing ability to turn life's miseries, like eating breakfast beans, into hilarious fun. I knew she missed Mom more than any of us, and yet she was determined to stay happy and funny, despite everything. Just hanging out with that baby cheered me up.

Dad wasn't handling Mom's absence nearly so well. He looked a mess—sleepy, sloppy, and deeply stressed about his meeting with Grandma, who, let's face it, was scary. Especially to Dad.

I don't want to suggest that Dad *only* cared about pleasing Grandma. He also cared deeply about Mom and all of us, and he cared passionately about important scientific questions. The search for alien life in the universe had obsessed him since childhood, as had black holes, dark matter, gravity, and all the other biggies.

But Dad needed Grandma to give him direction, to steer his genius toward practical things that people actually wanted. Dad loved robotics, but without Grandma he would never have invented Lil' Buddy the Walking Panini Press, both a pal and a sandwich maker all in one. Without Grandma, Dad might have written a lot of important papers about biology and DNA, but he would never have created his successful line of Poopless Pets, or Self-Chewing Nachos, or Napkin Pants. The list goes on.

The fact that only Grandma profited off his inventions, and that we had to live meagerly in a basement, didn't seem to bother Dad at all. He was happy just doing his work.

Like now, for instance, a look of profound satisfaction overtook him as he held up his newly completed Golden Hoop of wires. Kayla stared up at it too, but she did not look happy. In fact, I had never seen her so worried. Her face had grown white and rigid with fear.

"Dad!" she said, pointing at it. "What's the intended purpose of that invention?"

"Hmm, sweetie?" he said, looking over to her. "Oh, this? Just a little something I made for Mr. Abernathy, from the County Zoo. It's a security collar for a baby giraffe. See, a lot of animals have been going missing lately. Whole families of animals just disappearing. Everyone's upset and baffled. The police can't crack the case.

Your grandma thinks it would be great for the company if we solved the problem. We've had a lot of bad press lately. Something like this could really turn that around."

Talking about the Golden Hoop, Dad grew more animated. He began to look more like the Hap Conklin you would recognize from TV.

"Tigers, panthers, elephants," said Dad. "Whole animal families gone without a trace. And there's no sign of a break-in, no tracks, nothing on the security footage. Big mystery. Even the chief of police is stumped. But I think I've cracked it. The key is that *whole families* disappear . . ."

"Hmm," said Beth, glaring at Alice. "I hope the police don't come looking for any *known thieves* in the area."

Alice shrugged and went on eating. The fact that she didn't scream, "What would I want with a bunch of filthy zoo animals?" convinced me that she probably had nothing to do with the disappearances. But who *would* be stealing whole families of zoo animals?

"Wait, Dad," said Kayla. "You're meeting with this guy Abernathy *before* your meeting with Grandma?"

"Yes, at nine thirty." He looked up at the clock, which read 9:26. "Oh no! I should already be at the front gate! I haven't even attached the battery yet. I don't have time!"

"Don't worry," said Kayla. "Hap and I will go meet

Mr. Abernathy for you. That will give you a chance to attach the battery."

"Oh, could you?" said Dad, smiling with relief.

"No problem," said Kayla. "We'll bring him to the Crest Doors . . ."

I knew Kayla was up to something. I hoped she and Alphonso had figured out a way to trap Alice and get our stuff back.

"Come on, Hap," said Kayla. "Get your things. We're going to the front grounds."

"Okay!" I agreed.

First, I carried Baby Lu into the bedroom and handed her off to Eliza, then I grabbed my jacket and tie off their peg by my bed. I had to put these on before entering the front grounds, where Grandma insisted that everyone be "properly attired."

CHAPTER 9

SETTING THE TRAP

I found Kayla waiting for me outside.

"I'll get you your TV back today," she said. "But first you have to do one thing for me. You need to go to the front gate and meet Mr. Abernathy from the—"

"Whoa," I said, interrupting her. "Not just the TV. I want Squeep! too. I need that lizard back."

"Hmm," said Kayla, thinking. "Okay, the lizard too. But you have to do exactly what I tell you. Listen, this is very important . . ."

She started listing instructions. I missed most of them, because I was imagining myself returning to school triumphantly with Squeep! on Monday.

"You're not listening," said Kayla.

"Sure I am," I said. "What's all this about Mr. Abernathy, though? I thought you were trapping Alice."

"Uh, yeah," said Kayla. "It's sort of a . . . multiple trap. There's a lot more to this than just Alice. It's a volatile situation. Grandma's on the defensive. She thinks her enemies are closing in on her, and she's not wrong."

"You mean the FBI?" I said.

"Yes, among others." Kayla's eyes flashed at me. "Grandma's brought something here. For protection. A terrible creature to guard her secrets. Stay away from it, Hap. Stay out of the Black Room. That's where she's posted it to guard her secrets."

"Hey, I'm not going to go near any Black Room, or any other room of Grandma's, green, blue, or purple! What do you think I am, crazy?"

"You say that now," said Kayla. "But later on, you will stop listening to me. You will stop listening to reason, Hap. You change today. Look, it's happening already. You didn't shave this morning, see? You stop caring about the rules."

Touching my face, I found a full beard.

"You still care about our family, right?" asked Kayla.

"Of course!" I said.

"But you think you'd be happier without us."

"Well, I know I'd be happier!"

"Without us you wouldn't even be yourself."

"Then I'd be even happier."

This actually made Kayla stop and think a moment.

"Look," I said, "just tell me what I have to do to get my stuff back. I go meet this guy from the zoo, and then what?"

"Mr. Abernathy," she said. "Greet him at the front gate. Tell him you've come to take him to Dad. But don't bring him up the main path. Take him the longer way instead, through the garden. Stop at the iron gate and send him on to the Crest Doors, where Dad will be waiting. Now here's the most important part: do not follow Abernathy out of the garden. Instead, watch him through the bars of the iron gate. *Through the bars.* Do not take your eyes off him. I'll meet you there. Got it?"

"Got it," I said, wondering whether I would retain any of that.

"Good. Now I need to talk to Alice." Kayla turned and sprinted away.

"Don't forget about Squeep!" I yelled.

Then I hurried along the mansion's southern façade, buttoning up my dark-gray suit jacket.

Conklin Grounds was a truly spectacular landscape. The sight never failed to blow my mind. Flawless, tree-lined pathways crisscrossed an expanse of geometric gardens where every detail—every flower, leaf, and blade—expressed a harmony with the whole of Grandma's perfect design.

I hurried down the Grande Allée, a wide grassy path between ancient cone-shaped yew trees. There, I turned right at the fountain and ran toward the granite archways of the front gate.

A large man in a pressed tan safari suit had entered. This could only be Mr. Abernathy, the zoo guy. He stood surveying the beauty of Conklin Grounds with a look of delighted amazement. When his eyes eventually dropped down to me, he gasped, then let out a small scream.

I winced, realizing what a blot I was on the landscape. This was why I was supposed to shave. *Well,* I thought, *if this Mr. Abernathy doesn't like my beard, that's his problem.* He had a bushy little caterpillar-like mustache himself, and you didn't see me calling the cops about it.

"Mr. Abernathy?" I said.

"Yes uh . . . yes um . . . yes uh . . ."

"Yes indeedy-dandy?" I suggested. Sometimes I said weird stuff like this just to see how people would react.

"Um . . . um . . . ," he stammered.

"Please come this way," I said in my most butlerly voice. "We've been expecting you."

He hesitated, eyeballing me as he might regard something one of his animals had thrown up. As we walked together, he seemed to take my presence beside him as a personal insult. The distaste became mutual. I knew he had mistaken me for some kind of dwarf or adult little person. But so what if I was? Was that any reason to treat me so rudely? I realized Abernathy must be some sort of anti-adult-little-person bigot, and this made me want to shove him into the pond.

But instead I led him through the garden just as Kayla had told me to.

I tried to make polite conversation, but this guy could barely look at me without cringing. I returned all his cringes with smiles—smiles came easily when I imagined Abernathy falling into his tiger habitat and getting mauled.

"So you're a zookeeper?" I said. "You like animals and whichy-whats?"

"Uh, I'm the chief *director* of the County Zoo. And, uh, yes, uh, I find it rewarding—"

"Terrifico!" I yelled. "Nice mustache, by the way. So small, yet so bushy. That must be very rewarding as well."

"Um—"

"Splendid!" I said. "Well, right through this gate you can see the Crest Doors, where Mr. Conklin awaits you."

"Oh, thank God," said Abernathy, hurrying through the garden gate.

"Have a nice day," I said.

He spared me one last cringe, then hurried on. I regretted not shoving him into the pond.

Kayla had told me to watch him through the bars of the garden gate. Thick ivy covered most of this gate, but I found a bare spot in the greenery just about the size of my body. I figured this must be where Kayla wanted me to peek through. I pressed my face between two cold, black iron bars and watched Abernathy toddle along.

My dad, still holding the Golden Hoop, stood in front of the Crest Doors beside a young man named Chip Ricky, who was Grandma's personal assistant—a lean, elegantly dressed, pug-faced guy with an expensive leather clipboard. As Mr. Abernathy toddled toward them, I felt certain something very important was about to happen.

But nothing did. My dad and Chip Ricky shook hands with Mr. Abernathy, and the three men headed inside to conduct their business. That was it.

Who had we been trying to trap? I wondered.

A few moments later Kayla, holding her black-and-yellow backpack, strolled up on the other side of the bars from me.

"You just missed them," I said. "Should I have stalled Abernathy longer?"

"No, you did perfect," said Kayla. "Thanks for not pushing him into the pond. That couldn't have been easy. But it was the right choice."

Kayla and Alphonso didn't miss much, once they took an interest.

"Where's Alice?" I asked.

"She's already cooperating," said Kayla. "You'll get your TV back and the lizard too, though Alice has grown quite fond of him. I also made her give me something else that I think you should have." Kayla unzipped her backpack. "Hap, an FBI agent came onto the property yesterday. Alice acquired these from him, but they should really go to you. Here . . ."

I reached both hands through the bars to take what she was giving me.

Something silver, it felt cold on my wrists as it made a double-click.

"Hey!" I yelled.

Steel handcuffs now locked my hands together on the opposite side of the bars from my body. I was completely trapped.

"Sorry it has to be like this, Hap," said Kayla. "But I've reviewed all the futures, and this is the only way to stop you from going bananas."

CHAPTER 10

THE LAST HEXAGON

"I'm going to murder that bee!" I yelled, pulling against my handcuffs.

"Don't blame Alphonso," said Kayla. "It's my fault, really. I should have seen this coming earlier. But I didn't start to put the pieces together until this morning, when you asked me that question about Mom."

"What? What are you even talking about?"

"Grandma doesn't need for Mom to learn any more about laundry. She just sent her to that school to get her out of the way for a little while."

"Why?" I said. "And why did you have to trap *me*?"

"Because there's no other way to prevent you from breaking into the mansion today, but maybe—"

"That's crazy! I would never break in there!"

"You will today. It's inevitable. Alphonso doesn't lie.

But maybe you can do it without causing the Last Hexagon."

"The what?"

"The Last Hexagon. It's a possible future, an endpoint that I can't see anything past."

Kayla described the Last Hexagon to me. It looked like this:

THE LAST HEXAGON

DAD: IN FBI CUSTODY.

MOM: DEPORTED TO MOLDOVA.

ALL THE KIDS: IN FOSTER CARE, EXCEPT ALICE AND KAYLA, WHO WILL BE STUDIED IN A GOVERNMENT RESEARCH HOSPITAL.

"Okay, that sounds terrible," I admitted. "But there's no way I'm going to break into the mansion and cause that."

"There's no way you're *not* going to break into the mansion today. But maybe you won't cause the Last Hexagon. Maybe, if you break in before noon, and not after noon . . ."

"What happens at noon?" I asked.

Kayla hesitated, as though afraid to tell me.

"Today at noon," she said. "In the fifth-floor solarium, unbeknownst to Dad, Grandma will use that Golden Hoop he invented in an experiment on Baby Lu and—"

I saw it in my mind before Kayla finished her sentence: Grandma hooking those gold wires around the neck of sweet, smiling, innocent Baby Lu!

"No!" I yelled, pulling with all my strength to rip the cuffs apart. Unable to, I grabbed the iron bars and began shaking my body furiously against them. An anger so intense flowed through me that I felt strong enough to rip the whole gate out of the ground, and then I would charge into the mansion and run straight up to Grandma and . . .

Kayla waited while I thrashed uselessly until I had exhausted myself.

"Not Baby Lu," I said finally. "She's the only normal one of us left . . . What about the Safety Schedule? We need to tell Dad and—"

"Telling Dad leads to the Last Hexagon," said Kayla. "Calling the cops leads to the Last Hexagon. If I had told you without trapping you first, it would have led to the Last Hexagon. And if I had done nothing at all? You would have found out this afternoon, broken into the mansion to confront Grandma, and led us to the Last Hexagon. There's only one way to do this right, Hap. We only have one chance."

"Tell me."

"At 11:14, the Golden Hoop will be in Mr. Abernathy's possession on the third floor. At 11:16, he will leave it unattended on a marble table in the Azure Parlor, but only for about one minute while he goes to pee. If the Hoop vanishes during that minute, its disappearance will never be traced back to us. First Grandma will suspect Abernathy, then she'll suspect the FBI, but never us. That's our only chance of *safely* preventing the experiment on Baby Lu."

"So I steal it," I said. "At 11:16. Marble table. Azure Parlor. Third floor. I steal the Golden Hoop. Uncuff me. I'll do it. Unlock these things."

But Kayla refused to unlock me until I had memorized a bunch of directions—a lot of walking, counting, turning, running, and waiting. Kayla's timeline for me looked like this:

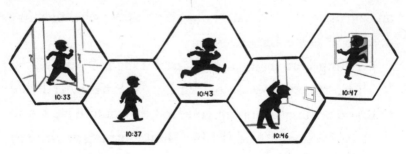

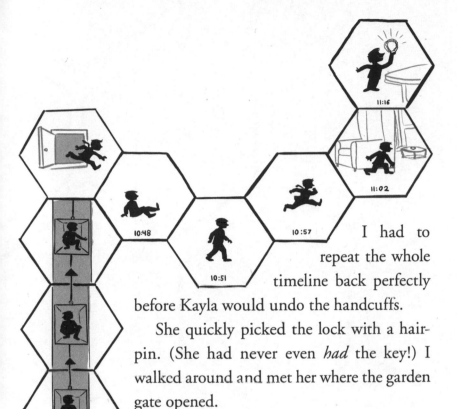

I had to repeat the whole timeline back perfectly before Kayla would undo the handcuffs.

She quickly picked the lock with a hairpin. (She had never even *had* the key!) I walked around and met her where the garden gate opened.

As we stared at the Crest Doors, cold fear rose up through my insides.

"Don't start walking until I say go," said Kayla.

Now my stomach dropped roller-coaster style. My head began to spin.

"Okay. GO!" said Kayla. "The timeline's started. Walk!"

Funny, there hadn't been anything in her predictions about me throwing up.

PART 2

HOW TO SELL YOUR FAMILY TO THE ALIENS

CHAPTER 11

THE MANSION

As I headed for the Crest Doors, Kayla walked alongside me for a while to make sure I was timing my steps correctly.

"One-two-three, one-two-three," said Kayla. "That's it. Good, Hap. Did you know this is a waltz rhythm?"

"Terrific," I muttered, still feeling lousy.

"The walking parts will be the hardest," said Kayla. "You're going to see things that make you want to run, or duck, or hide. Don't. There will be people everywhere. You'll be sure they're going to notice you, but as long as you keep this pace, I promise no one will see you. Don't start running until you're past the bearskin rug. If, for any reason, you fall off the timeline, just make sure you're in the Azure Parlor to get the Hoop by 11:16."

"Wait, if I fall off your timeline, how will I know when it's 11:16?"

"That's why I'm giving you this. As an emergency backup." Kayla pulled a small half-moon shape from her bag.

"Is that a taco?" I said.

"It's a frozen Clocko. Use it to tell the time."

"Ow! This thing is freezing." Turning the rock-hard taco over in my hands, I wiped a layer of frost from the small clock face on the tortilla shell. "Hey, this says it's four thirty."

"Yeah, the clock's broken," she said. "They really don't work very well."

"Then why give it to me?"

"Look, by 11:15 that thing will have melted enough for you to poke your finger through the queso down to the ground beef."

"Kayla, this might be the stupidest plan I've ever heard in my life."

"It will work!" she said. "Look, I've gotta go. I can't be here when the delivery guy comes out. Remember, don't run until you see the bearskin rug. And stay out of the Black Room!"

With that, Kayla took off sprinting west. I slipped the Clocko into my pocket, where it began freezing to the side of my thigh. A moment later, a preoccupied delivery guy came out of one of the Crest Doors, which began to drift closed behind him. I had to enter there before the door shut. So, of course, I wanted to run. But instead I kept walking, as Kayla had told me to, counting "one-two-three" between every step.

Never had a bearded boy been happier to see a bear-skin rug.

I had been *dying* to run! Once I passed the tail of that poor grizzly's hide, I took off like a sprinter. I could keep running now, according to Kayla's timeline, until I reached the Peacock Tearoom, whatever that was.

I ran onto mirror-polished marble that felt as slippery as ice. Past a fireplace the size of an overpass. Two uni-formed maids polished crystal glasses in a gold-framed mirror. *Don't slow down.*

I had worried that I wouldn't recognize the Peacock Tearoom, but you couldn't miss it. A room to end all rooms! It stopped me in my tracks, despite myself. Around beautiful treasures of gold, ivory, and turquoise, every wall shimmered like the purple-blue body of a peacock. Out huge windows, a jade-green garden grew flowers that matched the peacock colors so perfectly I shivered.

What on earth were we thinking going up against Grandma! The lady used real peacocks for wallpaper! Why were we doing this?

To save Baby Lu, I reminded myself, and hurried on. That wonderful baby deserved the chance to go through life without being experimented on the way I had been. She didn't have to be messed up like Alice, or the twins, or Kayla. Baby Lu still had a chance.

I summoned to mind the next moves of Kayla's timeline.

A nook in a far corner of the room hid a butler's station, and there I found the door to the dumbwaiter, just where Kayla had said it would be. A dumbwaiter, in case you don't have one, is a little elevator for food. It was also my ride up to the third floor.

I pulled open the door. But this was wrong! The little box inside was moving down. It was supposed to be moving up! Was I too late? Too early? Should I climb in anyway?

The box sank away. So I jumped onto the top of it, grabbed hold of the cable, and balanced on a little crossbar. Reaching up, I shut the door behind me and sank into narrow darkness, toward the basement.

My eyes adjusted. I listened to the echoing whir of the motor. What if I got caught in the gears? I needed to get off the crossbar and down into the proper compartment. But if I tried to slip down and the space turned out to be too narrow, I'd be crushed against the wall. I tried dangling one of my legs down, to see if I could fit.

Then the descent stopped. Light poured in an opening door. I yanked my leg up as the round face of Chef Van Dop came into view. He set a silver tea tray onto the dumbwaiter and polished its edges. The smell—Saturday cookies!—hit me like a truck. These were for Dad's meeting with Grandma. The cookies! *All the cookies.*

Chef Van Dop shut the door, leaving me in a dark sauna of aromas, hotter and fresher than I had ever known possible. Special Dutch cookies: pecan Jan Hagels, caramel *gevuldes*, and chocolate-butter *stroopwafels*. The tray was close enough for me to touch it. I felt suddenly ravenous. I hadn't eaten anything but beans for weeks! The gears whirred, and I began to rise. *Don't do it*, I thought. Grandma will notice even the smallest thing wrong with that tea tray. Do not do it. Don't weaken. Think of Baby Lu. Baby Lu.

I closed my eyes and felt at peace.

Then all at once, I thrust down my hand, swiped up a *stroopwafel*, and plunged it widthwise into my mouth. The flaky blazing hot chocolate-butter tasted so delicious that tears overflowed my eyes and rolled down my cheeks.

"Curse you, Grandma," I sobbed, licking my fingers. "Curse your *stroopwafels*."

I might have eaten another, but I noticed a door with a large three written on it passing by. The third floor! I pushed the door open and dove out, falling farther than I had expected, onto a dusty old carpet. This must have been the only dirty room in the house. It hadn't been cleaned in fifteen years.

I stood up, brushed the dust off my suit, and looked around at Dad's old room. A spaceship-shaped bed had the words "USS *Conklin*" painted across its side. It was the room of a kid completely obsessed with astronomy, space, and alien life in the universe. Well-worn encyclopedias lined the bookshelves, and a framed picture showed youthful Grandma holding infant Dad. After Grandma threw Dad out, she had closed the door on this place for good, as though unable to face the loss of the boy he had been.

I hurried out and shut the door behind me, but my thoughts remained on Dad, and his inventions, and Grandma. What had Dad said the Golden Hoop was *for* again? Zoo security? Something about giraffes? Why would Grandma experiment with it on Baby Lu? And what would it do to her? And where the heck was I?

By Kayla's timeline, I was supposed to be in the Chartreuse Vestibule. But this was just some yellow hallway! I must have made a wrong turn.

Up ahead, a pug-faced man hurried into the hallway, walking toward me while looking at an expensive leather clipboard. Chip Ricky! Grandma's personal assistant.

This could not be right!

Without thinking, I turned and ran in the other direction.

The moment I did so, I could almost *feel* Kayla's timeline rip apart into fluttering pieces. As I ran, I imagined Alphonso the Bee following me into some new passageway of hexagons that Kayla had never even considered.

I turned left into an open doorway and bumped into a small robot. A Lil' Buddy the Walking Panini Press. I had to reach out and catch it before it tipped over, or else it would have made the most ungodly loud clattering crash. Righting it back onto its flex-foot blades, I felt terrified that it would start bleeping and blooping and cooking panini. But, luckily, it appeared to be completely powered down.

I put a hand to my chest and felt my heart kicking to get out.

I stood in a wood-paneled office. At the far end was a closed door with a black doorknob. Closer to me, an office desk.

The nameplate on the desk made me gasp.

"Chip Ricky."

I had cornered myself! I turned around, peeked back into the hallway, and here came Chip Ricky, strolling toward his office.

Wheeling away from him, I again ran straight into Lil' Buddy the Walking Panini Press. This time it SMASH-BANG-CLATTERED onto the floor. No way Chip Ricky hadn't heard that!

I sprinted across the office to the other door. It was locked, but it was the kind of lock I could open by turning a button on its black doorknob.

I ran full speed into a room too dark for me to see anything.

Oh God, I thought, *I'm in a black room*. Was I in *the* Black Room?

I turned back toward the door. Into that wedge of illumination stepped Chip Ricky, looking horrified to find the door open. He leaned forward into the blackness.

The room was too dark for him to see me. But he wasn't looking, he was *listening*. Now I listened too.

We heard the low, deep breathing of an enormous—I mean *enormous*—animal.

Kayla's words from earlier replayed in my mind: *Grandma's brought something here. A terrible creature to guard her secrets. Stay out of the Black Room.*

Chip Ricky looked relieved to hear the creature breathing—whatever it was hadn't escaped.

Then he shut the door.

In total darkness, I heard its lock *click*.

CHAPTER 12

THE BLACK ROOM

Out of the darkness came a fearsome smell—a raw, predatory muskiness, like the reptile house at the zoo, but with a sickly-sweet, almost fruity, odor underneath. I was in the one place Kayla had told me to stay out of. Not only had I entered the Black Room, I had gotten myself locked inside. *Locked* inside with . . . What had Kayla called it? Some *thing* that Grandma had posted to guard her secrets.

From the enormity of the creature's breathing, I thought it must be a brontosaurus, or something comparably large. Listening in the dark, I found one reason to be optimistic: the breaths came in such a steady and measured rhythm that I believed the monster might be asleep. Maybe I could find a way out without waking it.

My eyes had adjusted to the darkness, but I could still see no farther than the nearest wall, a yard away. So, with infinite care, I began creeping along this wall hoping to find an unlocked door. The wall displayed prototypes and advertisements for secret or banned inventions—the sorts of things that Grandma needed to keep hidden.

A poster showed my dad pointing to a cylinder that flashed light. On it was the familiar Hap Conklin logo, but the ad's text was printed in crazy dancing blob letters unlike any foreign alphabet I had ever encountered. What did this light-flashing cylinder do? And  why hadn't I ever seen this invention before?

I crept on, carefully listening for any disturbance in the brontosaurus's breathing. Along the wall, I next saw a large flat-screen TV topped with a tall and curiously elaborate golden antenna that looked a little like the Eiffel Tower.

I was careful not to touch the TV. But it must have been fitted with some kind of sensor device that made it turn on whenever someone stepped in front of it. Because, to my horror, bright light and blaring sound erupted. I reached out and began fumbling along its edges for the off switch.

On the screen, my dad spoke from inside the mirror of a silver makeup compact, just like Alice's. This was a fomercial for the product tested on Alice! An hour ago I would have given anything to see this. Now I would give anything to shut it off. My hands fumbled around the TV's edges, searching for the off switch.

My fingers must have found the mute button, because the audio cut out, though the visuals played on. Listening, I could no longer hear the steady rhythmic breathing, and I knew the monster had awoken.

I turned around. The TV now lit half the Black Room, but I still couldn't see any creature. I scanned the walls for a second exit. I spotted a small door. It looked like another dumbwaiter, a few yards beyond a dark wall in the middle of the room. But then this dark wall began to move.

It was not a wall, but something as big as a wall lurking in the shadows.

The musky reptilian smell grew stronger, along with the sickly-sweet odor underneath, like . . . coconut body oil? From high above me, a deep giggling rolled out of the dark.

Then a new sound hit me so hard I had to plug my ears. The worst noise I had ever heard—not a shriek, but something happier and more evil than a shriek. A whoop.

No, I thought. *It can't be.*

Out from the shadow stepped two long red wrestling boots. Gator-skin leggings hugged thighs the size of tree trunks. A muscular torso like the cab of a truck. Last from the shadow came the insane and grinning face of Florida Pete, the world's strongest man.

"No way!" I said.

"Hot dang!" said Pete, stepping toward me. "I get to kill me another one."

"You're Florida Pete," I said.

"And you the second little FBI feller I caught in two days," said Pete. "The boss lady gonna be real happy with old Pete."

"No . . . ," I said weakly.

"Don't worry," said Pete, reaching down. "I'll kill ya nice and quick."

Some strange fear-instinct kicked in. I *punched* Florida Pete! In his leg.

Another deep giggle rolled down at me like tropical thunder.

"Is you crazy, little man?" laughed Pete. "You gonna fight *me*? I've had turds bigger than you today, John Law."

"I'm not John Law," I said.

"You FBI, sure as shoot. You look just like that last little FBI detective. Funny thing . . . I never thought they'd send another midget."

"Dwarf," I said. "Midget's offensive. And I'm not one. I'm—"

"I mean, sending a midget after a midget? Is that some kind of FBI mind game?"

"*Dwarf*," I said, "and I'm not one. I'm a—"

"That last little feller, Detective Frank Segar? Put up one heck of a fight for a midget."

"Dwarf."

"This here's all that's left of him."

Pete tossed me something, and I caught it without thinking. A small wallet. Opening it, I saw a tiny little badge. I felt queasy. An FBI ID showed a photo of the man Pete said he had killed—a bearded, adult little person named Frank Segar.

"Yeah, keep it," said Pete. "I threw the rest of him into the incinerator. And now I'm fixing to do the same to you."

Pete reached for me.

"Kid!" I yelled. "I'm a kid with a beard!"

Pete paused. Stooping down, he lowered his huge coconut-oiled face over mine.

"Hmm," he said. "I've wrassled with midgets in my day . . ."

"Dwarves," I said.

"And you don't look like much of a midget."

"Dwarf," I said. "Or little person."

"You look more like a kid with a beard."

"Yes!" I said. "I *am* a kid! With a beard. The boss lady? She's my grandma. My name's Happy Conklin Junior."

"Sweet corn fiesta!" yelled Pete. "Your daddy's *the* Hap Conklin! Why, he's my own personal hero. His fomercials are what started me fitnessizing. Changed my ding-dang life."

"Really?" I said.

"Sure did. I was one of the first-ever customers for Buns of Abs. Looky here." Pete turned around and pulled down his gator tights to reveal spandex Buns of Abs corrective pants. He started flexing the ab muscles on each buttock alternately, while saying, "Left flex! Right one! Left one! Righty! Lefty! Boom! Pow! Boom-boom pow . . ."

"Ah," I said. "Those are uh . . ."

"Pow-pow boom! Boom-boom pow! . . ."

"Very impressive," I said. "Hey, Pete? Uh . . . would you mind doing me a favor? Could you show me the way out of this room? And then maybe not tell anyone that you saw me?"

"Hmm," said Pete, hitching up his gator skins. "I can meet you halfway on that, partner. I won't tell no one you was here, but I can't let you leave this room until after I've killed you."

"Wha?" I said. I could see he wasn't joking. "Why? Why . . . kill me?"

"Have to," said Pete, stepping toward me. "Fighting and killing is all that's in my nature anymore. I try to be good, but the badness in me beats the goodness every time. It ain't even a fair fight. The only kindly thing I can do is kill you as fast as possible."

"Wait!" I yelled as he reached down for me. "What about my dad? He's your personal hero! You're going to kill your own hero's only son?"

"Your daddy is my hero," said Pete, pausing. "I have deep respect for all his hard work and innovation. And it couldn't have been easy on him having a midget."

"Dwarf."

"But if your daddy himself was here right now, I would have to kill him too. I'm powerful sorry about it, but my nature's become a hundred percent homicidal. Like a mighty hurricane. Beyond my or any earthly power's control. The only one who can wrangle me at all these days is the boss lady."

"Grandma."

"She's all that keeps me from killing every dang opponent who gets into the ring. She promised that when I reach the highest level of champion, she'll give me my *re*ward. An invention that will free me from my own brutality forever."

Strange, I thought. Florida Pete was already the world champion. How could there be a higher level than that? But then the mention of the "*re*ward" gave me an idea. If I could promise Pete the thing he most wanted in life, maybe he wouldn't kill me.

"*Re*ward?" I said. "What *re*ward?"

"Aw, it's too complicated to explain," said Pete. "Easier just to kill you."

Pete lunged his hands down at me. I twirled away, imitating once of the dance moves that the Masked Flamenco had used to evade him.

"Hey!" yelled Pete. "Stop that now, ya hear?"

He ran, clawing down at me like a tiger after a twirling rabbit. I tried to dance to the little door, which I hoped was a dumbwaiter, but Pete caught me. His hands clutched around my rib cage and felt like a tightening vise. Then the floor spun away as Pete lifted me high above his head. He bent me slightly at the waist in preparation for his famous double-suplex body slam, which would snap my spine like dental floss.

"Hold up!" yelled Pete, pausing mid-suplex. "Look! That's IT! Right there!"

Lowering me slightly, he pointed at the muted TV that I had turned on earlier.

"That's my *re*ward," he said, carrying me toward the television, which now showed an old fomercial for Hap Conklin's Perfect-O-Specs. It must have predated the FBI's involvement with that project.

"Your *re*ward's Perfect-O-Specs?" I asked Pete, who nodded happily.

In the ad, a series of miserable, unattractive schlubs put on the green Specs and looked at beautiful, fit people. Model types. In a flash of green light, the schlubs' bodies became shapely just like those of the perfect people. The model types would look briefly annoyed at having their identities stolen, but then they'd befriend the former schlubs for fun activities of the sort enjoyed by twins in gum commercials.

I recalled how just yesterday I had wished for a pair of Perfect-O-Specs, so I could have a body like Florida Pete's.

"Pete," I said. "I have to ask . . . Who are you going to look at with the Specs? I mean, who do you want to turn yourself into?"

Pete smiled wistfully.

"Something that will free me from my violent nature," he said. "Something sweet and gentle and lovin' that can live a hundred and fifty years without hurting a soul. Yup. A beautiful sea tortoise."

"What?" I said. "Really? You want to be a turtle?"

"A beautiful *sea tortoise*! And live to be a hundred and fifty years old!"

Pete whooped happily.

"But you wouldn't have hands," I said.

"I'd have flippers."

"But . . . have you thought about this, Pete? You couldn't even walk upright."

"I could swim and eat sponges."

"You could do that now!"

"Look, they ain't no comparison. Pete the sea turtle would never visit harm upon a nice feller like you. But Pete the man is about to snap your ding-dang neck."

"Wait!" I said, sensing my last opportunity. "If you just want the Perfect-O-Specs, I have a pair of them on me."

"You HAVE THEM?" Pete gasped.

"Right here in my pocket, unless you crushed them with those big mitts of yours."

Looking horrified, Pete released his grip on me, dropping me to the floor.

"They're right here . . . ," I said, going through my pockets.

If I have one real talent, it's the ability to pat myself

down pretending to look for something that I don't actually have. Unfortunately, you can only keep this up for so long before people grow suspicious. "Here they are," I said. "No, wait . . . I put them over here . . . No, wait . . . Hmm. Oh, I got them now! Right here," I said, pulling the frozen Clocko from my pocket.

"Catch!" I yelled, tossing the Clocko between Pete's legs into the darkness behind him.

Pete spun around and ran after it.

I bolted for the little dumbwaiter door in the wall.

"Hey!" I heard Pete yell from behind me, but he was too late. I flung open the small door and, diving into darkness, reached out both hands to grab the elevator cable.

In the next fraction of a second, I realized several things at once:

There was no elevator cable because this was not a dumbwaiter. It was an empty chute that fell straight down forty feet into orange fire. Pete's words came back into my mind, *I threw the rest of him into the incinerator.* Grandma had equipped her room of secrets with a means of destroying evidence in an emergency—an incinerator chute.

And I was falling straight toward the fire.

CHAPTER 13

GIFT HORSE

Falling toward a jagged black shape silhouetted above the flames, I held out both hands instinctively to block it from hitting my face. *Thwack!* The thing swatted hard into my palms. I gripped my fingers around it and held on.

I now hung, with both hands, from a long strip of metal—a torn piece of the chute itself, peeled down like the skin of a banana. Illuminated by the light of the fire below me, I could see how something had ripped the chute open here. Not "something," but "someone." All around the dark opening were small handprints in what I knew must be dried blood.

I remembered what Pete had said about the FBI agent. How he had "put up one heck of a fight." It looked like he wasn't done fighting. The man had somehow caught himself here, ripped open the metal chute, and escaped.

As scary as his dark exit appeared, it looked a lot more inviting than the fiery incinerator below. Pulling myself hand-over-hand up the strip of metal, I crawled into the small space. I had to stand up and walk sideways to fit along a narrow path between two walls.

For once, I was glad to be such a shrimp. The passageway would have been too tight for a normal adult, but not for . . . What had Pete said his name was? Detective Frank Segar. I still had his wallet, I realized. Silently, I thanked Detective Segar for the gift of this escape route. Then I realized that somewhere in this dark passage I might encounter the injured FBI man in person. The thought did not comfort me.

A thin crack of light appeared to float in midair up ahead. As I approached it, I began to hear something . . . classical guitar music. When I reached the light, I saw that the glow crept in from below a hinged flap upon the wall. It looked almost like an old mail slot. When I lifted the flap, two beams of yellow light pierced the darkness from two small holes about an inch apart. Eyeholes? Without thinking, I pressed my eyes up to the two openings and peeked through.

My mouth fell open in horror. Below, not three feet away, stood Grandma herself!

In a beautiful lavender bedroom, Grandma stood balanced on one leg, doing some sort of Tai Chi exercise. She wore a sporty black-and-red outfit.

Scanning the room, I spotted an antique clock, which read 11:00.

I had fifteen minutes to get to the Azure Parlor and steal the Golden Hoop. But the sight of Grandma, inches away from me, froze me to the spot. I couldn't even breathe.

The view, through a gorgeous wood-paneled bay window, showed we were on the second floor. But I already knew that Grandma's bedroom was on the fourth floor.

Did Grandma have *two* bedrooms? No, I decided, this room could not be hers. It was far too innocent and girly—all lavender and peach with a big satin-canopied princess bed. A large, framed photograph on the wall showed wild white stallions running through a river.

Grandma's arms weaved slowly above her head, her fingers tracing delicate little patterns in the air. While I didn't recognize what sort of martial arts, or dance, or witchcraft she might be doing, there was something familiar about it. Especially when she snapped her fingers.

A loud knocking at the door almost gave me a heart attack. Grandma clapped twice above her head, and stomped her foot. The music stopped on command.

"Come in, Mr. Ricky," said Grandma.

Chip Ricky entered, clutching his leather clipboard, and bowed.

"Ms. Conklin," he said. "I've brought the ones you wished to see."

"Show them in and go away," said Grandma, dismissing him with a weary gesture.

Chip Ricky exited and, to my astonishment, one of the twins entered.

I knew it was Eliza, first from what she wore, the purple sweater she had on this morning, and second by what she carried in her arms, Baby Lu. It was still her turn on Baby Lu's Safety Schedule.

Eliza, looking dumbfounded and terrified, averted her eyes from Grandma. Baby Lu gazed around in wonder—oohing and aahing at surroundings more beautiful than anything she had ever seen. When Lu caught sight of Grandma, she grinned lovingly—a smile of perfect innocence, from someone who had not yet learned about all the evil that existed in this world.

Do something! I screamed at myself. But what?

Follow Kayla's plan. Go to the Azure Parlor. Steal the Golden Hoop. I looked back at the antique clock. It still read 11:00! Why wasn't it moving? Why wasn't *I* moving? I couldn't tear my eyes away from the sight of Eliza carrying Baby Lu straight toward Grandma.

"Eliza, my dear," said Grandma, smiling. "How good of you to come. Oh, and look at this little angel."

Grandma reached out for Baby Lu, but Eliza pulled the baby away from her grasp.

"No," said Eliza. "Sorry. I mean, uh, it's just that it's my day to watch her. You know?"

A look of fury flashed across Grandma's face, but then she forced a smile. "Of course," she said. "I understand completely."

"Uh . . . ," said Eliza. "Why did you want to see me, Grandma?"

"I wanted your opinion," said Grandma. "One thing I've noticed about you, Eliza, is that you have excellent taste. I can see it in the way you dress and carry yourself. You have a natural eye. So, as one woman of taste to another, tell me, what's your opinion of this?"

"My opinion of what?" asked Eliza.

"Why, of this room, of course," said Grandma. "What do you think of it? As a bedroom, I mean? What's your general impression?"

As Eliza looked around, she swayed a little, as though lightheaded. I realized now that room had reminded me of Eliza from the moment I saw it. It looked like what she might have been trying to picture in her fantasies but could never quite visualize.

"It's so . . . exactly . . . perfect," Eliza said.

"See, I knew you had good taste," said Grandma. "It's so pleasant and peaceful here. The view is perhaps the most splendid in the manor, after the solarium's. That canopied bed belonged to the home's original owner. As did the bureau"—now, to my horror, Grandma turned toward me and swung her hand up so close I felt the wind of her gesture upon my eyes—"as did this charming oil portrait of Man o' War, history's greatest racehorse."

Eliza looked up at me. Paintings of horses didn't blink, so I tried not to either.

"Wow," said Eliza. "It is so . . . alive."

"Quite," said Grandma. "And of course there are the excellent Persian carpets."

"It's all wonderful," said Eliza.

"So glad you think so," said Grandma. "I've often thought it must be difficult to be a twin and have to share everything, including a room, with your sibling. So please accept this bedroom as my gift to you."

Eliza gasped. I thought she might faint. Her greatest wish was being granted.

"You may come and go in Conklin Manor as you please," continued Grandma. "Make use of our excellent domestic staff and kitchen services. You'll find Chef Van Dop to be among the finest in the world."

"Oh," said Eliza, panting and smiling uncontrollably. "Oh, oh! Thank you, Grandma. Thank you so much."

"Of course, my dear," said Grandma. "There is one little favor I must ask of you first. A very small favor, but one that must remain a secret, even from your parents. I'll need an hour or so to become better acquainted with darling Baby Lu here. It will give you the chance to get accustomed to your new room, and to get better acquainted with your new things."

"Bapy," said a little voice.

I saw now that Baby Lu was staring straight up at me.

"Bapy," she said again.

"What is she saying?" asked Grandma.

As Baby Lu lifted her arm to point, I shut the eye flap and stepped back into the darkness.

Run, I told myself.

But I took quiet sideways steps at first, until I could no longer hear the voices in the room. Then I ran—well, a sideways version of running, more like a gallop really— through the narrow path between the walls of Conklin Manor.

Get to the third floor, I told myself. Azure Parlor. Golden Hoop. Maybe I wasn't too late.

I had galloped maybe thirty yards when something collided with my thigh, and my body spilled forward into daylight. I tumbled out of a broom closet on a second-floor landing.

Leaping to my feet, I sprinted up the stairs to the third

floor. There, I found myself back in the yellow hallway where I had earlier encountered Chip Ricky. Racing through it, I doubted that even the real Man o' War could have run any faster.

Finally, the Azure Parlor came into view. I crossed a blue carpet and walked up to the marble table where Kayla had said the Golden Hoop would be.

The table was empty.

Behind me, I heard someone clear his throat.

I spun around and found myself facing the zookeeper, Mr. Abernathy. Frowning at me from a blue chair beside a blue-tiled fireplace, he clutched protectively at something in his pocket.

CHAPTER 14

THE ZOOKEEPER

"Ah, Mr. Abernathy," I said, as butlerly as I could. "Madam Conklin sent me here, uh . . . to see if you require anything. Refreshment-wise or such."

"No she didn't," said Mr. Abernathy, scowling.

"Oh . . . I assure you—"

"What are you supposed to be, anyway? A butler? Where's your name tag?"

"My what?"

"All the staff here wear ID tags. Everybody but you." Mr. Abernathy stood up.

"Ah," I said. "I seem to have neglected to put on my name tag."

"No you didn't," said Mr. Abernathy, stepping toward me. "You don't even look like one of the butlers here. You look like some kind of . . . strange little dwarf-man who's up to no good. Sneaking around. Poking his nose into other people's business."

Abernathy grabbed the poker from the fireplace and swung it at me like a cutlass. He bared his teeth as he stepped forward with the poker, as though eager to impale me. To my left there was an open window, and for a moment I considered leaping out of it.

"Tell me who you are," said Abernathy. "Or so help me, I'll crack your little skull."

"I'm sure I have my ID here somewhere," I said, patting myself down. As I mentioned earlier, I have a great talent for going through my pockets pretending to look for items I don't actually have. This time, however, as I mimed searching for an ID I didn't have, I found I actually did have one! A new inspiration dawned.

"Last chance," said Abernathy, jabbing. Then he paused and looked confused.

"Hey," he said. "What's so funny? What's the joke?"

"You're the joke, Abernathy," I said, laughing deeply. "But maybe you're not quite as dumb as you look."

"What!" he said.

I lifted the wallet, flipped it open, and showed him the badge.

"Detective Frank Segar," I said. "FBI. Now drop the weapon."

All the color drained from his face. As he stumbled

backward, the poker fell from his hand onto the rug. His bugging eyeballs began flicking around the room.

"Gonna make a run for it?" I said. "We have a team at every exit."

He let out a small yip, and his legs began to buckle underneath him.

"Sit down," I said. "Before you hurt yourself."

He sank back into the blue chair. *Wow*, I thought, *he sure looks guilty of something*.

"Hey, man," he said, breathing heavily. "I have nothing to do with these Conklin people. I don't even know what's going on here."

"Save it, zookeeper," I said, stepping closer. "We got it all on tape."

"Oh no," he cried.

"We got digital," I said. "Video. Reel-to-reel. We got DNA, Abernathy. D-N-A. Yup . . . it looks like you're headed for a different kind of zoo, to live with a different kind of animal."

He lurched forward, clutching his gut and covering his mouth as though he might be sick.

"Now, I'm only going to ask you this once," I said. "Where is it?"

"I can give you things," said Mr. Abernathy, looking up desperately. "I don't have money right now, but I can give you very valuable things."

"I only want one thing," I said.

"How about a panda?" said Mr. Abernathy. "A young, healthy panda. Worth a fortune."

"I don't want a panda."

"Snow monkeys," he said. "If you make this go away, I'll give you seventeen brand-new snow monkeys. Do you know how much those go for?"

"I don't want . . ." I trailed off as something occurred to me. Though I had only been in law enforcement for about a minute, already I had solved my first crime: Mr. Abernathy was stealing the animals from his own zoo and selling them . . . But why? I reminded myself that I was here for another reason.

"Give me the new invention, Abernathy," I said. "You know, the Golden Hoop."

"That? You don't want that. It's cheap junk. Worthless. How about a walrus?"

"I don't want a walrus!" I yelled. "Besides, you're a zoo-keeper! You're supposed to take care of those animals. Not sell them, or give them away as bribes!"

"I know I screwed up," said Abernathy, suddenly sobbing.

"Nice tears," I said. "You learn that from one of your crocodiles?"

"I know I messed up," he cried. "But I'm in deep trouble with some very bad individuals. I mean . . . I gotta survive."

"What about the animals!" I yelled. "Why don't *they* get to survive?"

"Whoa, Detective, you got it all wrong. I wouldn't sell to poachers or lowlifes."

"Who else would buy stolen animals?"

"These guys are pure class. They're, uh . . . like naturalists."

"Naturalists?"

"You know, scientist-like. Gentlemen hobbyists. A-OK. Wouldn't harm a hair. They'll look the species over, take a few notes, some innocent snapshots, and send them home in a week. Classy. Two, tops. Good as new."

"You must think I'm pretty stupid, Abernathy."

"I swear! The proof's right here."

Abernathy reached into his left front pocket and handed me a small metal cylinder.

"See?" he said.

It was the device advertised on the strange poster in the Black Room. It had a picture of Dad on it and a logo and lettering in the crazy foreign hieroglyphics.

"Keep it," said Abernathy, smiling and winking at me. "I didn't even see you take it. Doesn't have to go into evidence. Our little secret."

"What is this thing? What does it do?"

"Anything and everything. With these boys, the sky's the limit. Heh, not even the sky. Heh-heh. There IS no limit. Name your heart's desire and blammo. Money. Cars. Pandas . . ."

"How's it work?"

"It's a Flash Beacon. You hold it up and press the top."

"Is it drugs?"

"What! No, these guys are the real thing. They come to you. Wherever you are. Get you out of any pickle."

"Could they come right now?" I asked, thumbing the cylinder's cap.

"No!" yelled Mr. Abernathy. "Not while I'm here! See, these naturalists and I, there's a . . . miscommunication I'm in the process of smoothing over. So if it's all the same to you, I'd rather not use the Flash Beacon until everything's resolved. Uh, heh-heh. Heh . . ."

Behind me, a clock chimed the tone for the half hour.

Wheeling around, I saw the antique timepiece hanging upon the wall. It read 11:30. Far later than I thought!

"Where is it?" I yelled, turning back toward Abernathy. "Where's the Golden Hoop?"

"That?" said Mr. Abernathy. "The old lady has it. She said she had to take it up to the solarium to run some sort of test on it. At noon."

"Get down on the floor," I said. "Put your hands behind your head."

Abernathy did so quickly—before I had figured out what to say next.

"Now count to seven thousand," I said. "And I better not hear you stop."

To the sound of the zookeeper counting, I tiptoed quickly out of the room and back toward the yellow hallway. But there I saw two security guards walking straight toward me.

I ran back through the Azure Parlor and past Mr. Abernathy, who still lay counting on the floor. The security guards would be here before he had even counted to fifty.

I looked at the open window. What other choice did I have?

CHAPTER 15

EVERYTHING OUT THE WINDOW

Stepping out onto the windowsill, I gazed up the blocky facade stones of Conklin Manor. They looked almost climbable here. But could I make it up two stories to the solarium? And in time to stop the experiment?

I thought of Baby Lu. And those wires. And Grandma.

Taking a deep breath, I reached into the crevice between two stones and lifted myself up.

I had daydreamed about scaling these walls. From the ground it seemed doable. But distances that look friendly from below can turn on you from above. You face wind, vertigo, and the cold, hard fact of a three-story, unsurvivable fall.

My fingers soon went completely numb, and I felt too terrified to lift my weight on digits I couldn't even feel. So I wrapped my palms around a green copper downspout and climbed it like a gym rope. This brought me a few feet higher. An S-curve in the pipe took me near a fourth-story window ledge. But not near enough. I had to swing back and forth on the pipe a few times before I dared risk letting go.

My feet reached the ledge, but my body weight did not.

Falling backward, only a hip-rocking dance kept me from dropping to my death.

As I regained balance, I looked through the window. I saw Chip Ricky and Grandma coming out of the elevator. Grandma was holding Baby Lu.

"*Hap*," hissed a voice from above me. "*Hap*."

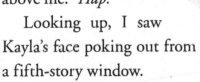

Looking up, I saw Kayla's face poking out from a fifth-story window.

"Get up here," she whispered. "Climb. Hurry."

With hands that felt like they had already fallen off at the wrists, I climbed and climbed.

Kayla grabbed my jacket and helped pull me over the window ledge. For a moment I couldn't catch my breath. We stood in some sort of flower-planting room.

"Kayla," I breathed. "What are you doing here?"

"I came to stop you, you idiot," she said.

"Stop me from what?"

"From flying us straight into the Last Hexagon," she said, and shoved me hard in my chest. "What are you going to do next, Hap? Steal the baby back from Grandma? Then what? How will you sneak Lu out of the mansion? Carry her out the fifth-floor window?"

"I would never do that," I said. "Did Alphonso say I would? Because I would never—"

"You have no idea what you're capable of anymore. You've gone some new breed of bananas. *Diving* into the incinerator? Punching Florida Pete? Impersonating a federal officer and history's greatest horse? You've become a reckless, unpredictable maniac! Putting everything at risk. Pulling us into futures too crazy to even contemplate!"

"So what do we do?" I asked. "How do we stop the experiment?"

"We *don't*," said Kayla. "We missed our only safe chance."

"But we can't just let it happen. An experiment on Baby Lu?"

"At this point, that's the least worst outcome I can see, as bad as it is. Because you trying to stop it, Hap, means the Last Hexagon."

"You traitor!" I said, backing away from her. "Baby Lu still has a chance, Kayla. She doesn't have to be a freak like us."

"I am not a freak," said Kayla, walking toward me. "For your information, I like being different. *You're* the traitor, Hap. I actually *like* our family. I like Dad not being arrested and Mom not being deported and me not living in a research hospital."

"I won't let any of that happen," I said, backing into a marble hallway.

"How can you *possibly* prevent it?" she said, walking toward me.

"You'll help me," I said. "Come with me. Help me find a new way through this."

Kayla scowled. Then she sighed.

"The problem is I can't keep stopping you forever," she said, following me into the hallway. "But there's nothing I can see down this way except disaster."

"Nothing you can see *yet*," I said, leading her toward the bright enormity of the solarium. "But keep looking, okay?"

"Every new prediction," she whispered, "is worse than the last one."

"Don't worry," I whispered back. "You're with an unpredictable maniac."

Kayla gave me the hairy eyeball. I led her down the marble hallway.

But soon she was the one leading me. We crept along the circular floor's edge, on a curving pathway between the latticed glass walls and a small forest of plants and statues. The tropical vegetation smelled almost violently intense. Between trees and sculptures of Roman emperors, I caught glimpses of Grandma walking with Baby Lu in her arms.

Beyond a small fishpond, where a young sea turtle peacefully swam, Grandma carried Baby Lu to the center of the circle and set her down on a pedestal.

Kayla led us so close I felt sure Grandma would hear and look up, but she did not. We crouched behind a little banana tree. Grandma lifted the Golden Hoop and fastened it around Baby Lu's neck.

I tensed up. Kayla squeezed my arm as though to say, "Not yet."

Little lights came on all over the delicately braided gold wires.

"Wait," breathed Kayla.

Grandma turned and walked out of the room.

"Now," said Kayla.

Leaping up, we ran around the fishpond. Baby Lu

smiled as she saw us approach. I put a finger to my lips. Kayla lifted her up from the pedestal. I could still hear Grandma's heels clicking somewhere nearby.

"She's coming back," I said.

"I know," said Kayla. "We need to hide."

She pointed toward an antique carved wooden chest.

"Won't she find us in there?" I asked.

"Yes," said Kayla. "But it will buy us a few minutes to think until she does."

I ran and opened the lid of the chest.

"Quick. Get in," I said. Kayla stepped in with the baby.

"Hurry up, Hap," she said. "Come on, get in too."

"No," I said. "I need to talk to Grandma."

Kayla stared at me. Her face quivered. Then she gasped,

as though some new possibility had dawned. Her eyes filled with tears.

"What do you see?" I asked.

Turning away from me, Kayla reached down and unfastened the Golden Hoop from under Baby Lu's chin. Then she lifted it to me and wrapped it around my own neck. As she fastened it, a tear rolled down her cheek. Then she hugged me, as though for the last time.

She crouched down into the trunk with Baby Lu and began to close the lid over them.

"Go do it, Hap," she said, just before the lid shut.

CHAPTER 16

GRANDMA

I turned around in time to watch Grandma stride back into the room. Finding the pedestal empty, she stared down for a moment in confusion. But her features calmed as she heard my footsteps approach. She flashed a cold smile.

"Happy Junior," she said before looking up at me. "I might have known."

"Hi, Grandma," I said. I walked closer, my eyes locked on hers.

"So," she said. "Our little bearded revolutionary. Have you come to overthrow the tyrant?"

"I just want to talk to you," I said, stepping closer.

" 'There is a tide in the affairs of men,' " said Grandma, " 'which, taken at the flood, leads on to fortune.' But perhaps, young man, you have misjudged that tide."

"Uh . . . okay," I said. "But, Grandma, you are not going to experiment on Baby Lu."

"*Experiment* on her?" Grandma laughed. "I should say not. I have never experimented on any of you. I will protect her, as I have protected all of you. And, yes, as I have gifted each of you with your own special greatness, so I shall gift Baby Lu."

"Ha!" I said. "Protected us? Gifts? Special greatness?"

"Indeed," said Grandma. "The inventions have only ever been pretexts to make you each exceptional and worthy of your destiny."

She's lying, I told myself. *Don't believe a word she says.*

"I made each of you extraordinary," she said. "Just as decades earlier, when your father was a baby, I gave him the gift of his unique genius."

This stopped me. My blood ran cold. It had never occurred to me that Grandma had experimented on Dad. *She's lying*, I told myself. *She's trying to trick you.*

"Even if I believed you," I said, "I would still not let you near Baby Lu. First, because she's already great. And second, whatever you do could go wrong. Like with Kayla."

"You think Kayla's greatness is an *accident*?" said Grandma. "Does Kayla seem like an *accident* to you? She's one of the most remarkable people on this planet. Granted, she's not perfect yet. She worries and hesitates far too much. She's like the poor cat in the adage, letting 'I dare not' wait upon 'I would.' Quite unlike *you*, Happy

Junior. I made sure that you would be brave, bold, and decisive. Manly, even before your time."

"Me?" I said. *Don't listen to her tricks*, I thought. *She lies about everything.*

"You think your beard is just a nuisance, yet you fail to see that with it, I have given you strength and valor in an almost equal portion to my own. You don't even realize yet how powerful you are. But I have something here that will help you to achieve your true greatness."

Grandma reached into a pocket of her sweater and pulled out a tiny box, wrapped in glittery black paper and tied with a blood-red bow.

"With this, you can fulfill your destiny to be my partner in a great endeavor."

She stretched her hand toward me, as though she wanted me to take it. "Join me, Happy Junior. As a *partner*. And together we shall win an extraordinary victory for humankind."

"Thanks," I said, stepping closer. "But I don't want any more of your 'gifts.'"

Grandma scowled and dropped the box back in her pocket.

"As to a 'partnership,'" I said, "sure. Fine. I'll do anything you want. On one condition: Baby Lu gets to stay normal. No gifts or greatness or specialness for Baby Lu."

"Normal," said Grandma. "What is normal? Take a look at this."

Grandma pulled the rose from her lapel.

"Do these petals look normal?"

I noticed a coil of pink electricity dancing atop the red petals. As I leaned in to see better, she pushed the rose toward me, touching its electricity to the center of my chest.

The pain started big and only got bigger, until it was too enormous to feel at all.

"How dare you!" said Grandma. "I offer you my hand in partnership, and you spit conditions in my face?"

Numbed to my core, I could neither feel nor move but only sway a little, like something badly balanced.

"I am deeply disappointed, Happy Junior. To think I ever imagined us as a team. I must be going soft in the head. My offer is officially revoked."

Now a larger coil of pink electricity bloomed atop the rose, and Grandma jabbed it straight into my face.

I didn't feel the floor, even as I collapsed upon it like a bag of soccer balls. Grandma continued to talk to me, but all I could hear now was the crazy quivering feedback the electricity had left in my head.

I strained my hardest to move even one single finger, but my brain seemed not to know what a finger even was, let alone where one might be found.

"One more," said Grandma through the feedback, "and you will learn the lesson."

No! I thought as the rose in her fingers flowered up into a blaze of red fire.

Fingers, I told my brain, *the five things at the end of the arm. Those things that feel covered in a billion pinpricks. Yes, those.* Aiming the flower down toward me, Grandma noticed my hand flopping and jerking to life. I reached into my pocket and pulled out the Flash Beacon. Her mouth formed the word "don't" as I raised up the cylinder and pressed the button.

CHAPTER 17

THE "NATURALISTS"

The Flash Beacon vanished into pure light. My hand was empty.

Otherwise, it didn't seem like much had changed. I still lay on the floor of the big bright solarium, but now the only sounds were the faint motorized hums of my gold collar and the filter in the fishpond. We remained the same two people in the same positions, but I realized an important difference: Grandma, who had been moving, was frozen, and I, who had been frozen, could move, though not much or well.

Piece by piece, I heaved myself up from the marble floor. I felt awful, like I had some weird tropical disease and the ambulance coming to save me had run me over instead.

I heard a *clop*.

From where? It hadn't come from the fishpond.

A few seconds later, I heard another *clop*, then a

clop-clop, a *clop,* a *clop-clop,* a *clop,* and then so many more *clops* that recounting them all here would get monotonous. I looked off toward the *clops,* through a high doorway into the adjoining room. Something in there kept clopping. From above the doorway, a long, slender yellow shape slinked down—a shape of orange patches on yellow. I didn't recognize it as a neck until a giraffe's face showed up at the end. Ducking down, the giraffe came clopping into the solarium. Other giraffes followed. All of these giraffes, I noticed, wore jade-green glasses on their faces, like Beth's Specs, only larger.

"Ack," said the giraffe, spotting me. "Here he is! I found him! Ack! This way, everyone! He's in here. Ack!"

I screamed.

You would have too. I know talking animals in stories are magical or funny, but in real life they're upsetting. You get nausea and nightmares. Because things that shouldn't talk *shouldn't talk.* Right?

"Ack," said the first giraffe. "Ack. Hello."

I screamed again, which upset several of the giraffes.

"Could you, ack, not make that sound, please, ack?" said the leading giraffe.

"Stop talking!" I yelled. "Oh God!"

"I'm sorry, have we, ack, done something to upset you?"

"You're giraffes! GIRAFFES!"

"We are not, ack, giraffes, if that is the problem. Ack. We have merely chosen these forms so as not to alarm you."

"Well then, you have chosen *badly*!"

"You are not 'not alarmed'?"

"If I was any more not 'not alarmed' I'd be leaping out the window!"

The giraffes looked perplexed. There were about twenty of them now. A medium-size one began whispering to the leader. The leader then raised his right front foreleg and lowered his face all the way down to it so he could make some adjustments to his Specs with his hoof.

Then he aimed the Specs at me. Jade light beamed out from the lenses and scanned me like a yogurt at the supermarket.

"It seems we have made an error in, ack, synthesizing," the giraffe said, "due to, ack, conflicting information. We detected the communi-ack-cation center of a human. Yet our strongest readings from you are those of the very giraffe species you find so, ack, frightening."

I started screaming again. I couldn't help it.

"All right, ack," said the giraffe. "Our apologies. We shall make our, ack, appearance something more familiar."

Now all the giraffes aimed their specs at me and scanned me with jade light.

Then the giraffes began to change.

Their necks deflated—giraffe heads falling left and right—their bodies stood upright and shrank and they all grew beards and suddenly the many giraffes looked identical to . . . me.

"Ack. This is better?" asked the leader.

"NO!" I yelled. "Put some clothes on!"

More scanning, then *whoosh!* They wore clothes like mine. The beings all had bright, intelligent expressions, but otherwise they looked just like me.

"I'm sorry about the confusion, ack," said the me who had been the giraffe who said "ack" a lot. "You are the one who called us, ack, here, right?"

"Uh," I said, trying to remember.

"Ack, the rest of us will be able to talk as soon as we ack-ack-acclimate."

These were the naturalists that Mr. Abernathy had told me about when he gave me the Flash Beacon. He had said they could get me out of trouble. I looked toward my grandma, who stood as still as the Roman emperor statues surrounding her.

The one I had started thinking of as "Ack" stepped toward Grandma.

"Is this the being who will be visiting us?" he asked.

"Visiting you?" I said.

"We don't have enough time for this," said a different one, finally able to speak. "We must not acclimate too much to these strange bodies."

"Ack. Let us not be rude, Gubbins," said Ack, and then turning to me said, "Please let me, ack, introduce myself. I am Gubbins. This is Gubbins, and Gubbins, and Gubbins, Gubbins, Gubbins . . ."

To save time I'm just going to tell you that they were all named "Gubbins" and they were all completely identical, except that one said "ack" a lot, which I took to be some sort of hiccup or speech impediment.

"So," I said. "You guys are, like, aliens, right?"

"Well," said Gubbins. "Isn't everyone an alien in some context?"

"Sure, sure," I said. "But you guys are, like, ALIENS, right?"

"Ack, yes," admitted Ack. "Normally we, ack, wouldn't

have to ask who you are, but we can't seem to get any clear reading on your identity."

"Well," I said. "My name's Hap Conklin Junior."

A murmur of excited recognition ran through the Gubbinses.

"As in *the* Hap Conklin?" said one. They all smiled as they remembered how famous the name was, and then frowned as they remembered why.

"Confirmed!" said one of the Gubbinses. "This is Hap Conklin."

"Junior," I said.

"Well," said Ack, trying to smile but looking a little sick, "we are, ack, *very* familiar with your advertisements."

"Those aren't mine. They're my father's."

"Ack, but we love your Panini robot," said Ack.

"Those aren't my products," I said.

"Your advertisements are very annoying," said another, still not understanding.

"No," I said. "Not me. I'm Hap Conklin *Junior*. My father, Hap Conklin *Senior*, makes that stuff."

The Gubbinses stared back with such blank incomprehension that for a moment my face looked normal on them.

"He's the father," I said. "I'm the son. We're totally different guys. Understand?"

They looked at me as if I were from another planet.

Finally one said, "Hap Conklin, I have been using your fitnessizing products."

"They're not mine!" I said impatiently. "I am Junior, he's Senior!"

"Enough," said the impatient Gubbins. "We have no time to waste on absurdities. May we borrow this human or not? We will pay one million US human Earth dollars, in cash."

"Uh, borrow?" I said, following their eyes to my grandma. "For how long?"

"Our rate is always one million per unit per week."

"A million what? Dollars?" I asked.

The Ack Gubbins nodded. "Ack."

A million dollars and Grandma gone for a week. What a great deal! I could save Baby Lu and have enough time and money to free my family from Grandma's control. I felt sure this would also keep us out of the Last Hexagon that Kayla was so worried about.

Still, I hesitated. Something about loaning my own grandma to shape-shifting space Gubbinses didn't feel right.

But then I looked at her. I looked at the strange electric Taser rose with which she had so painfully zapped me. What was that line she had said to me a moment ago?

"There is a tide in the affairs of men," I said. "Which taken at the something something leads straight on to the good stuff."

"What does that mean?" said Gubbins.

"It means yes," I said. "Take my grandma."

"Sign here, please," said Ack, holding up a document written in those crazy hieroglyphics. "Your finger will do."

My finger wrote ink on that paper just as a pen would have. I signed my name.

"Transaction complete," said Gubbins.

Grandma started to vanish, while in her place bound stacks of hundred-dollar bills materialized. The bill bands around each stack looked like this:

"We will return the being in a week," said Gubbins. "We appreciate your business."

"Please let us know how we may serve you better in the future," said Gubbins.

All the Gubbinses but Ack began to fade.

"Ack, please," said Ack, staring up at the sunlight. "Can't we just stay, ack, a little longer?"

Gubbins looked at him in surprise. "You have acclimated far too much to this form! You forget yourself, Gubbins! You must come now."

"Ack! Just a little longer," said Ack, fading more slowly than the others.

"Now!" said Gubbins.

"So beautiful," said Ack, staring up at the dome of the solarium.

"Don't you have glass on your planet?" I asked him.

"Not the, ack, glass," he said. "Your sun."

"You don't have a sun?"

"We do. But Gubbins hasn't seen it for too long. Not for very many of your lifetimes. Ack. Such a long time ago."

"How long ago?" I asked.

Ack looked at me.

"Yesterday," he said, and then vanished.

CHAPTER 18

THE YOUNG MASTER

Yesterday? I thought as Ack disappeared. That didn't make sense. If Gubbins hadn't seen their sun in several of my lifetimes, how could they have seen it only yesterday? Could a single day on their planet last several human lifetimes?

And if so . . . for how long had I just loaned them Grandma?

"Wait!" I yelled. But Gubbins was long gone. Several questions now bothered me at once. There had been so many Gubbinses, but how come it now seemed like there had been only one? How could so many different beings all have the same name? And why hadn't Gubbins been able to understand the concept of my dad and me being different people?

I realized that Kayla would know the answers.

I ran to the carved wooden trunk and opened the lid. But Kayla and Baby Lu were not inside. Instead, there were twenty more bound stacks of hundred dollar bills, like the one where Grandma had been, and two more copies of the strange document that I had signed with my finger.

After staring down for a while, I started banging my hand on the bottom of the trunk to see how they might have slipped out. But it was completely solid.

"Hey!" yelled a voice. "What are you doing there?"

Spinning around, I saw Chip Ricky entering the room.

"Where's Ms. Conklin?" he demanded.

"Uh . . . ," I said, pointing at the pile of bills "She *was* right there."

Crossing to Grandma's black pedestal, Chip Ricky snatched up the document I had signed.

I turned back to look in the trunk, at the other two piles of money.

"Kayla," I said, unable to breathe. ". . . and Baby Lu . . . and Grandma."

"Vanished, have they?" he said, still reading the receipt.

I nodded.

"Your father signed *this*?" he said.

"No," I said. "That's my signature."

"You can read Gubbinsglopf?" said Chip Ricky.

"No . . . I mean . . . Wait, *you* can read that?"

"Most of it," said Chip Ricky. "We recently had Florida Pete sign a similar contract. We've only been in business with these beings for a few years."

"What? . . . But why?"

"After Earth governments banned our products, Ms. Conklin asked your father to find alternative markets for the inventory. So, I've had to familiarize myself with such contracts before. The general gist of this one seems to be that you have sold your family to the aliens, though I'm not at all sure how that's possible."

"No! I just loaned them Grandma for a week."

"These aliens," he said, "have no distinction between individuals and their families. So, if you sold them your grandmother, the rest of your family would be sold as well. The only irregularity I see is how you yourself are still here. Since you are part of the family that you have legally sold to them, they should have taken you as well. That's quite puzzling."

He stared down at me a moment. Then he snapped his fingers and pointed at the collar around my neck.

"The Golden Hoop," he said. "The security collar! I guess it works."

"What?" I said, reaching up and touching the Hoop around my neck.

"See, they always take whole families," he said. "It's just like the animals in the zoo. Whole families disappear . . . Your father invented the collar to keep the animals safe from abduction. And now, the collar has kept you safe."

"No, but I . . ."

"If you don't mind me saying, Mr. Conklin, you have played your cards brilliantly. Conklin Manor, Conklin Industries, and the entire estate are now legally yours. The Conklin holdings on Earth alone are worth billions!"

"What?" I said.

"Hmm," said Chip Ricky, consulting the spreadsheet on his clipboard. "We'll need a new laundress, of course."

"Mom!" I said. "But she's in Nevada!"

"Your entire family will be taken by the aliens. Geography is unimportant in matters of teleportation. So, Mr. Conklin, shall I assemble the remaining staff to meet the new young master?"

Turning away from him, I headed for the stairs.

I ran all the way down to our rooms in the basement.

There was a pile of money where each of my family members had disappeared. I supposed there was a pile of bills somewhere in Nevada that had been my mom.

If I could have gathered them for a family portrait, it would have looked like this:

I stood in the door between my family's two small rooms in the basement.

I noticed that Dad had swiped three cookies from his meeting with Grandma and left them for me on the kitchen table.

Kayla had kept her promise, too. The TV sat on my cot, plugged in and ready to watch.

She had gotten Squeep! back for me as well, just as she said she would. He sat on my pillow in front of the television screen.

Still numb with shock, I sat down on the cot beside Squeep!

The bedroom seemed impossibly still and quiet. I looked at my TV, at the plate of cookies, at the lizard—all the things I had wanted.

I began to cry.

Then I began to panic.

But you can only cry and panic for so long, before you realize that you need to take action.

I had to get my family back, from wherever they were.

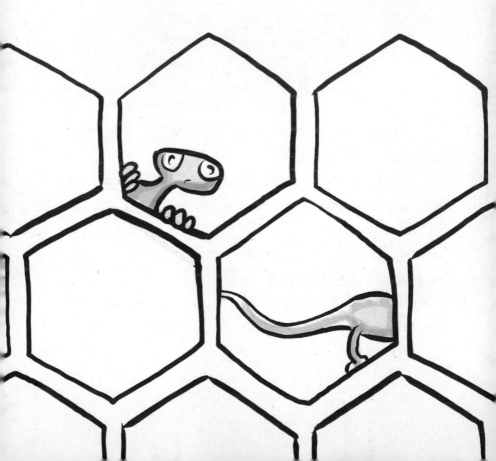

PART 3

SO YOU'VE SOLD YOUR
FAMILY TO THE ALIENS

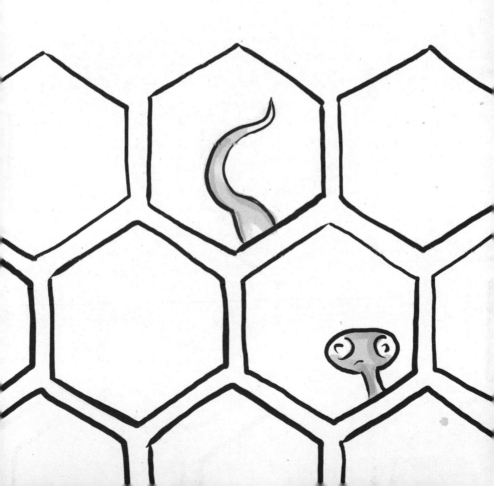

CHAPTER 19

LISTEN TO THE LIZARD

I didn't like the way that Squeep! kept staring at me.

"What are *you* looking at?" I said.

He held me in his cold lizard glare, as though accusing me of something unspeakable.

"What?" I asked. "Do you think I *wanted* to sell them to the aliens? You think I somehow planned this whole thing? Why would I?"

He gazed back icily, silently. He was sweating me like some kind of reptilian district attorney.

"What did I stand to gain from it?" I said. "I mean, besides money and . . . everything I ever wanted. So what if I said I would be happier without them . . . people say a lot of things. At least I'm doing something to get them back! Unlike you, you lizard."

I held up the notebook, where I had been writing down

my rescue plan for the past several hours. I looked over what I had so far:

BUY A ROCKET FROM NASA.

"Okay, I know it's not a very good plan," I said to Squeep! "But do you have a better one?"

Squeep! ran over to the TV and began whacking his tail against it. He had very expressive body language for a lizard.

"You want to watch TV?" I said. "How's that going to help?"

Shaking my head at him, I went back to my notebook. The problem with any rocket plan was that I didn't even know where in space my family was. They were probably light-years away—somewhere inaccessible to man.

Think harder, I told myself. *Focus!*

Squeep! wasn't helping. He kept whacking his tail against the TV.

"Would you stop that?" I barked.

He became sad and downcast. I felt terrible for snapping at him.

"I'm sorry, Squeep!" I said, picking him up and hugging him. "I shouldn't have yelled at you . . . You're the only family I have left now."

This made me suddenly emotional. I began rocking Squeep! in my arms and singing him an old Moldovan lullaby. He bit my finger.

"Ow!" I yelled, dropping him back onto the cot. He ran back to the TV and started banging his little head against it.

"Why do you want to watch TV so badly?" I asked.

Looking at the set, I noticed now that Alice had attached something new to the top—a little gold tower antenna, like the one I had seen on the TV in the Black Room.

Curious, I reached out and clicked the set on. The moment I did so, Squeep! looked deeply relieved, as though thinking, *Finally!*

As the set warmed up, I began eating one of the *stroopwafels*.

I heard the music for *Wrastlinsanity*. Only it wasn't *Wrastlinsanity*, but some kind of sci-fi horror movie with the same sets, graphics, and sounds as *Wrastlinsanity*. It even had the same deep-voiced announcer, though instead of English he spoke some burbling gibberish language. And instead of wrestlers, hideous monsters fought.

This giant bug monster . . .

Fought this flying spiked eel monster . . .

. . . in all the most brutal and gruesome ways imagin-
able. I couldn't believe they allowed stuff like this on TV!
The incredibly scary flying spiked eel monster defeated
the giant bug not by pinning it, but through multiple dis-
memberments and decapitation.

As they played the *Wrastlinsanity* victory music, the
graphics showed the spiked eel monster at the top of

the championship bracket. Its next challenger would be a team of furry, bug-eyed spider monsters.

The animated bracket scrolled down to promote an upcoming match. To my surprise, I saw that one of the next fighters would be Florida Pete! They had Pete chained up and imprisoned in some kind of glass pen. The world champion thrashed wildly against his steel chains but could not break them.

Announcing this next match, the deep voice said the equivalent of "Aaand the chaaallenger!" in the burbling gibberish language.

A camera zoomed in on the challenger, which was not a monster or a wrestler at all but eight terrified human beings: My mom! My dad! My five sisters! And Grandma.

I spit cookie crumbs everywhere.

My family was in this death match! They were making them fight. Those lousy, rotten, double-dealing Gubbinses were making them fight!

Imprisoned in a glass pen, huddled together in horror, my family stared up at something that cast a strange violet light down upon them. Only Kayla stared straight at the camera—straight at *me*. She mouthed the same inaudible words over and over: Ah . . . Oh . . . Ee. Kayla was trying to tell me something.

Ah . . . Low . . . Ee. Fah . . . Oh . . . Eep.

Follow Squeep!

She wanted me to follow Squeep! Wait, where was he?

I saw that the lizard had leapt off my bedding and scrambled over toward Alice's cot. I stood and followed him. Squeep! had wrapped his little front flippers around Alice's silver makeup compact. He was trying to lift it up toward me, heaving with all the strength in his exclamation-point-shaped body. I reached down and took it from him.

I examined the little disk of silver. Could Alice's secret hiding place still be connected to her? My dad had invented one technology that let beings cross the universe. Could the compact be another?

I pressed the little latch to pop it open.

Like magic, fancy script letters engraved themselves onto its silver surface and formed two words: "Access Denied."

This vanished and was replaced by more serious-looking text:

"Warning: Use of Doorganizer by unauthorized persons *will* be catastrophic."

I tried to remember what the fomercial I had watched in the Black Room had said about the Doorganizer.

"The Ultimate Closet Space Solution," I recalled. "Reads your DNA."

So only Alice could open it, because only Alice had Alice DNA.

I scanned the room for traces of Alice DNA.

My eyes stopped on her nightstand.

Oh no, I thought. *Anything but that.*

I walked toward her big hairbrush—the one she cleaned so seldom that it resembled a small red Persian cat. I picked it up.

In a day full of unpleasant experiences, what I did next might have been the most unpleasant.

Wincing, I pulled a big handful of her hair out from between the bristles. This I wrapped around my fingers like a mitten. I held the makeup compact in this hair-mittened hand and pressed its latch.

New words engraved themselves into the silver: "Accepted . . . Welcome, Alice."

It popped open so suddenly that I dropped it to the floor. I felt sure it would shatter into a million pieces, but instead it landed there, open. Its circular mirror shining.

Squeep! ran straight toward it.

"Wait!" I said, crouching

down toward him. As I watched him run toward his reflection, the Squeep! in the bedroom vanished, while one in the mirror remained, staring out at me.

As I squatted down to get a better look at this, my own reflection came into view *behind* Squeep!'s. The moment I glimpsed my own eyes, I felt the me in the bedroom disappear.

Squeep! and I were somewhere else, crouched on a different floor, staring out through a small circle at the world we had left behind.

CHAPTER 20

THE COMPACT

"**U**se of Doorganizer by unauthorized persons *will* be catastrophic."

From the moment I entered Alice's Doorganizer I *felt* the coming catastrophe. Every instinct in my nervous system told me to get the heck out of there, to somehow crawl back through the little mirror where we had entered.

I looked over at Squeep! He kept bobbing his head in a beckoning gesture, as though to say, "Come on, this way."

Against my better judgment, I left the little portal to normalcy behind and followed Squeep! deeper into what was simultaneously the largest, the smallest, and the strangest place I'd ever been. I felt a primal terror of the unknown.

I kept recalling that woman in the Doorganizer commercial.

Did this mean that even though Alice had left a compact behind, she still had another one with her somehow? Was Squeep! leading me to her current one? To another mirrored portal through which I could rescue my family, assuming they hadn't already been killed in the alien death match?

Blocking that last thought from my mind, I focused instead on following the lizard across the cedar-paneled floor. Squeep! scurried along through the piles of stuff that Alice had stolen over the years. I passed several of my old library books, Beth's favorite jacket, the family's collection of board games, my first-grade Big Wheel, my gym uniform, my calculator.

The sight of all my old stuff should have been making me angry at Alice, but instead, I realized, I had actually started to feel *sorry* for her.

She hadn't even unwrapped a lot of what she had stolen. Her compulsion didn't even let her enjoy any of it, beyond whatever momentary pleasure she got from the theft itself. What a terrible thing to have to live with.

"Holy moly," I said, taking it all in.

How could Alice have possibly stolen so much junk?

Kayla's beloved Raggedy Ann doll—the one she had made a little yellow headband for—lay on the big plastic slide that had disappeared from the school playground a few years ago. I saw Eliza's dollhouse, where she once had spent hours pretending that each room was hers alone. No sign of Beth's Specs, however. Most of the things in the loot piles I didn't recognize at all. Who knew where Alice had gotten so much weird stuff

As I gazed around in bewilderment, I realized that of all the weird things in the compact, the weirdest thing of all was . . . me. That place had changed me into something unfamiliar and given strange new abilities to my body and mind.

I could still move and walk around normally if I chose, but I could also go where I pleased without moving my body at all. I could look through the pages of my old library books without even moving my hands or eyes. Can you imagine what that would be like? You can? Good. Because here's the weird part:

I could also do the things I did in there *BEFORE I DID THEM*.

If that doesn't make any sense to you, how do you think I felt?

It happened like this:

I'd been standing there stupefied, unsure of my next move, when in the distance, I saw something strange on the ground. It looked like . . . a person. A person lying there on the floor! I wanted to walk over and see who it was. But the moment I decided to do so, the plan became a sort of *memory*, only one that went into the future instead of the past. I "remembered" ahead, how I would walk over to the person on the floor.

As soon as I "remembered" how I was going to do this . . . I had already done it, even though I still hadn't yet. I became two me's: the me who walked to the person *and* the me who hadn't yet. The me who had looked down and saw that the person on the floor was . . .

. . . ALSO ME!

But, like, a me from even farther in the future, a me who had gotten lost and grown old inside the Doorganizer. I hadn't gotten any taller, but my face had wrinkled and I had some gray in my hair. Far Future Me also wore a leather jacket exactly like the one I had always wanted.

Was Far Future Me dead?

I reached down toward him to check his pulse. My fingers touched his neck. His eyes sprang open.

Far Future Me grabbed my arm and flipped me over with an awesome judo move. He landed on top of me, pulled my arms behind my back, and began shouting and frisking me and pulling things out of my pockets.

"It's okay!" I yelled back. "It's just me. I mean, it's just you. I mean, I'm you, in the past, so it's okay."

He made a low wheezing sound. As he pulled me to my feet, I saw he was laughing.

"I'm not you, Hap," he said. "Don't worry. Although, I think you've been *pretending* to be me."

He held up the badge that he had pulled from my pocket.

"No!" I said. "Detective Frank Segar?"

"Uh-huh," he said, folding the badge into his back pocket. "You know, it's a crime to impersonate a federal officer."

I goggled at him in disbelief.

"What's wrong, Hap?" he said. "You don't look very happy to see me."

"It's not that," I said. "I just kind of thought that you were me . . . like me way in the future."

"You should be glad I'm not. It means you'll get taller."

I would have given up getting taller to be a cold-eyed guy in a leather jacket who knew awesome judo moves.

"How did you get in here?" I asked. "I thought this place only had stuff that Alice st— Uh . . ."

"Careful, Hap," said Frank, smiling. "You wouldn't want to say the words 'Alice' and 'stole' to an FBI agent."

For a guy who wasn't me, Frank sure knew a lot about what I was thinking.

"Look, I'll tell you all about it," said Frank. "But can we sit down first? I'm exhausted. I've been trapped in here for weeks, and this place keeps making me fall asleep."

"Weeks?" I said, sitting down beside him. "Florida Pete told me he just saw you yesterday."

"Maybe it's only been one day outside the Doorganizer," said Frank. "But time happens very differently inside a black hole."

"What?" I yelled. "We're in a black hole? . . . But how? Why?"

"'The ultimate closet space solution,'" said Frank. "It's the extra-dimensional space around a micro black hole. That's what our scientists think, anyway. Maybe it's really a white hole or a wormhole or a quasar or something. All I know is, it's illegal. I mean, can't your dad build a closet without endangering the stability of the universe?"

"But . . . ," I said as this all sank in. "How did you even get in here?"

"Long story," said Frank, yawning.

As he told me the FBI's side of things, Frank kept drifting off to sleep, and each time I shook him by the arm to wake him up. He said the Justice Department had been investigating my family since Dad invented the Perfect-O-Specs thirteen years back. But that the case hadn't become a top-priority matter until the zoo animals started disappearing last month. He didn't say how they knew Grandma was mixed up in that.

The FBI had known all about the Black Room and the incinerator. They knew if they raided the mansion, Chip Ricky could burn all the evidence before they got to it. That's when they called in an elite infiltration expert: Detective Frank Segar. They figured that Frank looked enough like me to pass through the servants' gate of Conklin Manor without drawing attention.

But Grandma, somehow one step ahead of them, had posted a guard in the Black Room: Florida Pete, the world's strongest man.

During their face-to-face encounter, Florida Pete had easily overpowered Frank's best judo moves and threw him down the incinerator chute. Catching himself halfway down, Frank improvised an exit through the mansion's wall—the same one I had used to make my own escape the next day.

"Wow," I said. "So after all that, you didn't even get your evidence."

"Who says I didn't?" said Frank. He reached into his pocket and removed a clear plastic baggie, which contained a familiar pair of green glasses.

"Beth's Specs!" I said. "You're the one who took them."

"They weren't what I came for," said Frank. "But they're still illegal. Enough for us to start making arrests and getting to the bottom of things. Only before I could get out of there, your other sister woke up and attacked me. Alice Conklin. I almost had my cuffs on her when she pulled me into this godforsaken place. She must have done the same thing to you, huh? Pulled you in here?"

"Uh . . . ," I said. "Well, something like that."

"Any idea when the little klepto plans on letting us out?"

"What if she can't?" I said. "What if she never opens the door and lets us out?"

"Huh," yawned Frank. "Then I guess you're going to spend eternity looking at a white midget in a black hole."

"Dwarf," I said.

"White dwarf, black hole, yellow moons, orange stars, what difference does it make?"

So far I hadn't told Frank anything about my own situation. Part of me really wanted to blurt the whole thing out. Maybe Frank would help me rescue my family. And for this job, a judo-trained infiltration expert might be just what the doctor ordered. Plus, I liked Frank. In a way, he had saved me from falling into the incinerator.

On the other hand, Frank seemed mostly interested in locking up my family and throwing away the key. Some of us probably deserved it. But for the rest of us it would surely lead to the Last Hexagon scenario that Kayla had been so worried about.

On the other-other hand, wouldn't my family be better off in an Earth jail than in their current situation?

As I weighed my options, Frank began snoring loudly.

A few moments later, Squeep!, who had been hiding, crept out from behind a pile of backpacks and stared up at me. He flicked his tongue out, accusatorially.

"What?" I whispered. But I knew what he meant. *Stop wasting time sitting around. We need to get going.*

I looked back at where Frank lay sleeping. I knew what I had to do. Frank had evidence that he could use against my family, and I couldn't let him keep it.

Carefully, I reached into Frank's jacket pocket and pulled out the evidence baggie with Beth's Specs inside. I slipped them into my own pocket.

You can judge me if you want. I know Frank was on the side of the law and everything. But in my heart, I was on the side of my family.

I tiptoed away after Squeep!, following his wending pathway between the piles and piles of stuff Alice had stolen.

Eventually, Squeep! and I came to another tiny mirror, the same size as the one we had entered through.

Squeep! hissed excitedly when he spotted it.

"Wait up," I said.

Ignoring me, Squeep! ran straight toward the little circle and then vanished. I crouched down to look into it. Again, it happened the moment my eyes met their own reflection. I vanished from the Doorganizer into a very different sort of place.

CHAPTER 21

WHAT THE ALIENS LOOK LIKE

Here's where Squeep! and I found ourselves:

Squeep! and I floated in low gravity in front of the silver compact we had entered through. The compact stood fixed in some sort of beam of light.

I surveyed the enormous room for any sign of my family. I saw many glass pens, all of which contained strange creatures, though no humans, let alone Conklins. I tried to turn all the way around to see behind me, but this made me so dizzy I thought I might be sick.

Squeep! swatted my face with his tail to get my attention. He flicked his tongue and waved his flippers back in the direction of the makeup compact. I had gotten pretty good at reading Squeep!'s body language and eventually figured out what he was trying to tell me. He wanted me to grab the makeup compact out of that beam of light so we could take it with us. But by the time I realized this, we had floated up so high the compact was out of reach.

I tried swimming back down to it. But you can't swim through low-gravity air the way you can through water. And trying to made me queasy. If I wanted to get back to the compact I would need to push off against something. I looked up beyond my legs and saw an architectural beam a few feet away, so I wheeled around to grab it.

Squeep! hissed angrily at me. He really wanted me to grab that makeup compact, and here I was going in the opposite direction. I tried to explain, through gestures of my own, that I only meant to float up a few feet so I could push myself back down again off the beam. But this was not an easy concept to mime to a floating lizard.

Our argument was interrupted by the sudden approach of a glowing, eight-foot-tall, giant-headed monster. It looked like this:

Its skin glowed with an indigo light. It did not seem to have noticed Squeep! and me floating there just above it. As it approached, I could feel the enormous weight of its body. The creature must have been made of something heavier than any Earth life-form. As it passed just below us, Squeep! and I churned through the air like dust motes in its wake.

Spinning wildly away, I grabbed hold of a ledge along the wall, which turned out to be the sill of a large window. I found myself staring out at the alien world. A night sky full of strange bubbly clouds above a cityscape teeming with the same sort of glowing aliens that had just passed me. Creatures heavy enough to walk in this low gravity instead of float, and all with giant heads and glowing skins of many different colors.

Quietly, I tried to turn my body back around to reorient myself. Across from me stood a glass animal pen containing a very different kind of alien that I recognized from the preview of the upcoming death match I had seen on the TV. I noticed how, like Squeep! and me, they floated and were a lot lighter than the native aliens.

I turned my body more fully around until I was looking down at that heavy, glowing alien again. It still hadn't noticed me clinging to the window about ten feet from where it stood. It took an instrument from its utility belt and began scanning around the edges of the silver compact, as though testing it for something. In addition to the belt, it wore a tunic and carried a satchel, both emblazoned with the writing I had seen the Gubbinses use.

I felt sure this alien was a Gubbins.

Then it put the instrument back into its belt. It reached one of its four hands toward the compact, as though it meant to take it.

Suddenly, Squeep! jumped out from behind the beam of light and bit the giant alien on its finger. The alien screamed—I assume more from surprise than pain. It shook Squeep! loose from its finger. Then it began swatting wildly with all four of its hands to knock Squeep! from the air. Floating backward out of range, Squeep! stuck his tongue out and hissed furiously.

The native alien glowed red with anger. It reached down into its belt and withdrew what could only be some sort of gun. It took aim at Squeep! and blasted out a bolt of lightning.

The bolt missed Squeep!, zipped past me, shattered the glass pen across from me, and then blew open a large hole in a window.

The air pressure changed violently. My body flipped around so hard that I nearly lost my grip on the window's ledge as the broken window began pulling me hard toward the dark bubbly sky.

I watched the furry creatures from the cell across from me get sucked through the hole like dust bunnies into a vacuum. I could see them screaming in the night air outside the building, where, I'm sad to report, they met a very unfortunate end. The atmosphere out there inflated

them like balloons until they popped. A horrible thing to behold!

I knew from the pressure pulling my body toward the hole that the same thing would happen to me out there if I didn't hold on. These glass cells were like fish tanks, designed to protect us exotic foreigners from the planet's real environment.

But to the native alien, still standing there holding the gun, this was all no more than a breeze. Creatures like it were made of stronger stuff that could survive out there.

I began growing lightheaded for lack of oxygen. Soon, I knew, I would lose my grip, get sucked out through the hole, and implode in the pressure. I cursed myself for not having thought to bring a protective spacesuit, or at least a fishbowl for a helmet.

But then I remembered I did have something that might protect me.

Letting go of the sill with my left hand, I reached into my pocket and pulled out the Perfect-O-Specs that I had taken from Frank Segar. Shaking them loose from the evidence bag, I hooked them over my eyes and stared at the heavy, glowing alien. It still hadn't noticed me. It stood there in the breeze, holding its gun and looking for the little creature that had just bitten its finger.

I clicked the button on the side of the Specs. A beam of green light scanned over the creature—like a barcode at the supermarket.

I felt the Specs growing larger on my eyes. But then I realized it wasn't just the glasses. My eyes and head were growing too.

But now my right hand lost its grip.

The force from outside yanked me up and out into the night. It flung me faster and farther than I could have imagined.

Just find them, I told myself as I began to black out. *Find your family*.

I woke up on a ramp surrounded by lights of a color I had

never seen before—a color I had never *been able* to see. I took the enormous Specs off my enormous face and put them into the strange satchel I now carried.

I tried to stand up, but I had too many arms.

Also, my flippers were asleep.

CHAPTER 22

GUBBINS

Yes, aliens have big heads. That's the one thing we got right about them.

But my big alien head didn't make me any smarter. As far as I could tell, the big head wasn't for thinking. It was for worrying about the big head.

There's an old alien saying:

"Watch the head!"

Or sometimes just "Head!"

The second set of arms, I assumed, was for head protection. But why the long extendable neck? The last thing I wanted to do with my big head was send it off into the path of who knows what. The huge eyes, however, were excellent. Like a fancy new TV, they made everything sharper and more colorful.

I set out straightaway to find my family. First, I needed to find a way back into the enormous building I had flown out of, which looked like some sort of domed stadium.

But all my ideas about maneuvering the alien body proved wrong. I wasted an hour flopping around helplessly, which might have drawn attention if there hadn't been so many others flopping around too. We were, after all, outside a large sports stadium, a location universally conducive to inebriated flopping around.

Most of the sky was the purest black I had ever seen. What faint light it had did not come from stars—there were none—but rather from enormous crisscrossing bands of strange clouds. Dark, churning, bubbly things, they appeared to be made up of perfectly round beads of all different sizes.

What are *those*? I thought, and I found my alien brain knew the answer. Those were not clouds at all, but *moons*, thousands and thousands of moons. These guys had more moons than they knew what to do with.

My alien brain knew a lot about these moons. For most of their history the aliens had called this planet by a name that meant "The Good Place Under the Moons." But in more modern times, after making contact with the native inhabitants of several of the larger moons, they had changed their planet's name from "The Good Place Under the Moons" to "No, *We're* the Planet!"

Apparently an argument had broken out about who lived on the actual planet and who lived on "Just Another Moon," a name we now applied to several of our neighbors.

My skin was mostly lavender. I had an orange mark in the shape of a ^ on my tunic.

Staring at this ^, I knew somehow that ^ meant "Gubbins."

Repeating the name to myself made spots of orange appear on my skin. I felt happy to see them. But, as fear and confusion returned, the spots faded to pale grays and blues.

My new skin changed colors a lot, and it didn't take me long to figure out that pale grays and white corresponded to fear, green to confusion, red to anger, orange to happiness, and the colors I had never seen before to feelings I had never felt before.

These changes weren't voluntary. I couldn't turn orange by trying to be happy any more than I could turn happy by trying to be orange. This must be a very honest society,

I thought, if everyone can know how you feel just by looking at you.

An indescribable color and accompanying discomfort
told me that I really had to go to the . . . I didn't know
what I had to go do. But I had to go do it BAD.

I let the body take over. My flippers flew me up one
ramp, then down another, and into a small private room,
where I relieved myself. I'll spare you the details.

When I set out again, I stayed on the wide, main-street
ramps that circled the great arena.

The city bustled with attractions and vacationers looking for a good time. This was typical of night-side border
towns a short distance from Morning.

My alien-self knew lots of things instinctively. It knew
that since a single day on this planet took over a thousand
Earth-years, only the super rich lived in the Day. The Night
housed its residents in ruins left by Daylight civilizations
long past. Towns like this one catered to rich tourists from
the Day, who came in search of the sorts of amusements
prohibited by Morning Law, like *Wrastlinsanity*, which here
meant captives from other worlds battling to the death
in the arena.

The arena, I thought. Wasn't that where I had been trying to go?

The more I acclimated to the body and let its instincts
take over, the easier everything became. Soon, I cruised

confidently along the ramps to the front gate of the arena.

Crossing under its arched entranceway turned my skin bright orange with happiness.

Inside, ramps branched toward many different levels of seating. Up beyond these ramps opened a vast domed amphitheater decked out in *Wrastlinsanity* lights and logos. Crowds had already started camping out in the stands for the next death match.

I knew that what I was looking for could be found on the levels below the arena floor.

Security guards, seeing the ^ symbol on my clothes, passed me through their checkpoints without question. I followed ramps marked "alien pens" downward to the floors below the arena's floor, where I entered a maze of compartments.

I could look down into the alien pens from the walkways that crisscrossed above. I found myself wondering about the best ways to free the aliens. But then I thought: *Why would I want to do that?* Aliens were dangerous and had to remain in captivity—a point driven home by the sight of the giant spiked eel monster swirling around in its massive glass cell—one of the most dangerous creatures in the known universe. Destroyer of all competitors! A champion worth a fortune. And I, Gubbins, owned it! Freeing it was the last thing I should want to do.

Continuing along, into a different gravitational habitat, I came to a different pit-like pen, which read:

"Humans—Conklins."

Looking down into this pen, I saw several units of the Conklin alien. But my mind only counted one being—an alien named "Conklin."

I found Conklin strangely familiar, and yet repulsive.

One of the smallest parts of Conklin, a form that wore a band of fabric around its head, looked up and stared at me.

Suddenly, I didn't feel good. Sickly blotches of conflicting colors popped out all over my skin. I turned the color of panic. I had to get out of there!

But then I heard comforting voices behind me.

"Gubbins," said one.

"Gubbins," said the other.

Turning, I saw two beings exactly like me. Both had the ^ symbol on their clothes.

"Gubbins!" I yelled.

I glowed bright orange as I flew toward them. I linked lower arms with them both, and they glowed orange too. At long last, I had found my family.

CHAPTER 23

FINALLY HAPPY

And so began the happiest time of my life.

For a Gubbins, being among family felt wonderful. I found every Gubbins fascinating, beautiful, and special. Because every one of them was my favorite person: me.

No Gubbins ever bored me. Any story they told was something new that *I* had done.

"That's brilliant!" I'd say, and then I'd savor the compliment.

Now and then, I would remember that I wasn't really a Gubbins, but an imposter on a secret mission. This realization turned my skin all the gray shades of guilt, sadness, and fear.

Seeing my distress, the rest of the Gubbinses would rush over and cheer me up, until I turned orange again and had forgotten whatever had been troubling me. In this way, Gubbins maintained perfect happiness for every family member.

Whenever I felt lonely, I would find a big group of them. And whenever I just wanted to be by myself, I would find an even bigger group of them.

I felt so proud of myself for being Gubbins, and so proud of Gubbins for being me.

Then suddenly I remembered my real name: Hap Conklin. I remembered that my real family, the Conklins, were about to fight in the arena. To the death! I had to save them all from being killed!

Why did I keep forgetting this? I turned red in angry frustration.

Seeing my change in color alarmed all the other Gubbinses. Not wanting my anger to contaminate the rest of them, they rushed over to tell me how much I meant to them. They praised and honored me until I turned orange and forgot about everything except how happy I was.

A few minutes later, I remembered who I was again. I hated myself for forgetting about my family. The sight of me colored taupe with self-loathing sent a pale ripple of panic through the whole Gubbins family. They swarmed me with embraces, affirmations, and presents, including my own Lil' Buddy the Walking Panini Press, a very popular item among the Gubbinses. It made me so happy that I turned bright orange and again forgot my real identity.

Around this time, Squeep! crept out of the shadows and tried to make contact with me. Not recognizing him at first, I wrapped him in focaccia bread and nearly made him into a panini. Luckily, at the last  minute, he stuck out his tongue, and I remembered him.

I set him gently on the floor and began following him through the different gravitational habitats. Now I know that he was trying to lead me back to the makeup compact, so I could take it to my family and we could all escape through the Doorganizer together. But at the time, I didn't even remember that his name was Squeep!, only that I was supposed to follow him for some reason.

Then I became so distracted by the sight of the glass pen holding Florida Pete that I forgot all about the lizard. Pete looked completely wild and out of his mind with adrenaline, thrashing and pulling against his steel manacles and shackles. I stared down at him, trying to remember how I knew this giant earthling.

Two Gubbinses arrived bearing a load of raw meat to

feed to Florida Pete.
Pulling open a chute
atop the cage, Gub-
bins began sliding
the bloody cuts
down a wide
glass feeding tube
to where Pete waited
greedily. My Gubbins
brain knew that this
meat contained lots of special additives and chemicals
that would make Pete more violent and uncontrollable,
which would create the best show possible, for what we
now called the Imperial Death Match.

In the short time since Gubbins had introduced *Wrastlinsanity* here, it had become the top TV program across
several solar systems. And this tournament would be the
greatest one yet, because the Emperor of the Galaxy himself would be attending in person! Emperor Galacto
Supremo had never even been to our planet before. Gubbins needed to make this the most thrilling spectacle of
blood and death in the history of the universe.

As I contemplated this, the other Gubbinses noticed
me turning a darker and darker gray.

"Don't worry," they told me. "The death match will go
fine."

Then, before my fear could infect others, they hooked me under the arm and pulled me back to the main group of Gubbinses, where a pre–death match party was in full swing. Soon, I too was bright orange again and singing and dancing all the classic Gubbins tunes of old.

A bit later, I found myself more or less alone and looking down into the Conklin Habitat. That's when, for the first time in several weeks, I saw my mom in person. She stood rocking Baby Lu and singing to her.

Reality hit me like a sledgehammer. I wanted to leap straight down to her, but I felt too ashamed about everything I had done—selling them to the aliens, choosing to be a Gubbins instead of a Conklin over and over again, and probably getting them all killed. I didn't deserve to be called a Conklin anymore, or her son, or Baby Lu's brother.

But I also couldn't stay up here, among the Gubbinses.

Taking the Specs from my pocket, I hooked them over my eyes and flicked the switch to "Undo."

The glasses, my head, and body all shrank down at once, until I was just ordinary Hap Conklin again in my dusty old suit. The only difference now was that my beard looked about three feet long.

I pulled open the hatch at the top of my family's cell and slid down the glass feeding tube like it was a playground slide.

My mom and Baby Lu were the only ones awake in

this part of the pen. Before I could express my sorrow and tell her how I didn't deserve to be in the family anymore, she looked at me and gasped and shouted with joy.

Running toward me, she lifted me up in her arms alongside Baby Lu.

"*Căci acest fiu al meu era mort,*" said Mom, "*și a înviat; era pierdut, și a fost găsit. Și au început să se veselească!*"

This meant, "I thought you were dead, but you're alive!"

But it sounds a lot better in Romanian.

CHAPTER 24

REUNION

The next family member I saw, I almost didn't recognize. She looked about Eliza's age, but had freckles like Alice.

"Beth?" I said, in amazement.

"Hap?" said Beth. She hadn't recognized me either at first, what with my long hillbilly beard.

Beth hugged me the moment Mom set me down.

"Wow," I said. "So this is the real you, huh? You look great!"

"Ugh, yeah," said Beth. "I hate it."

"Well, at least you're not a rat," I said. "I knew you guys were just fraternal twins."

"I wish we were identical," said Beth. "I can't get used to this, after looking like Eliza all my life."

"Well, I like you better this way. But I guess it's your choice now, since I brought you back these."

"My Specs! Oh Hap! Hap! You brought me my Specs!"

The others began rushing in, yelling my name and hugging me. Dad, Kayla, Eliza, and even Alice hugged me. Everyone except Grandma, who stood a ways off, staring at me sullenly.

"Look!" cried Beth. "Hap brought me my Specs!" She had already put them on and transformed herself back into Eliza's double.

"And my compact?" said Alice.

"Yes, Hap," said Dad. "We need the makeup compact."

"Where is it?" said Eliza.

"He doesn't have it," said Kayla.

"What!" yelled Grandma. "He didn't even bring the blasted Doorganizer?"

"But . . . ," I said. "I thought it was always connected to Alice."

"The aliens knew we could link hands and escape through it," said Dad. "So they found a way to separate it from Alice. I think they've trapped it in some sort of magnetic light beam."

I smacked both hands to my forehead. This was what Squeep! had kept trying to tell me—to bring the compact! It was our only way of escape.

"Oh bravo, Happy Junior," said Grandma. "Excellent rescue. Really superb. Now we'll all be brutally murdered, thanks to you."

"Don't even start with me, Grandma," I said. "This is all your fault."

"My fault?" said Grandma. "You're the one who sold us into bondage."

"I was just trying to protect Baby Lu," I said.

"Protect her from what?" said Grandma. "A Golden Hoop that would have prevented her abduction by aliens? Those Hoops would have protected all of us."

"But you *started* the abductions!" I yelled. "You sold the aliens the Flash Beacon! You sold them *Wrastlinsanity*. You created these death matches."

"Of course I did," said Grandma. "That was all essential to my plan. These depraved blood-sport tournaments. The decadent consumer goods. It's all designed for the same purpose: to sweep through this galaxy like a virus, softening the Empire, eroding its bonds of power, until it is weak enough to be taken over."

"Taken over?" I said. "By what?"

"By me, you idiot!" yelled Grandma. "By us! What do you think I've been working toward all these years—the perfect panini? As I told you, it was all by design. It was all to achieve the greatest possible destiny for this family. And it was working! Until *you* stuck your beard in."

Looking around at my family, I could tell that Grandma had already confided her big crazy plan to them during their captivity.

"I'm not acting out of selfishness," said Grandma, "or hubris. I just can't stand to see such a glorious galaxy ruled by *that* brainless twit."

Grandma pointed upward, toward a TV monitor mounted on the wall. It showed the vast arena packed to maximum capacity. All the aliens had turned toward an entering procession. The tens of thousands in attendance all bowed down at once, genuflecting before the Galactic

Emperor. The camera cut to a closer shot of the small waving figure. I recognized the face as the same one that had been on all those bill bands wrapped around the money.

"What an imbecile," said Grandma. "What a half-witted buffoon of an emperor. I would have been doing the galaxy a favor. If you don't believe me, ask Kayla. She knows which future would have been better."

I had forgotten about Kayla. I spotted her standing in the corner and making little faces to herself as she talked to Alphonso.

"Kayla," I said. "When will they make us fight?"

"In twenty seconds," she said, "the ceiling will open. The floor will rise, lifting us into the arena."

"Is that big spiked eel thing up there?" I asked.

"We'll never make it to *him*," she said. "Florida Pete will kill us all in the first round. Grandma will last the longest against him."

"Wait," I said. "Can't Grandma control Pete? He told me she could."

"No, he's too jacked up," said Kayla. "He'll rip Grandma to pieces before he even recognizes her scent. He'll rip us all to pieces."

Grandma shook her head at me in disgust.

"Why couldn't you have just brought that damned compact?" she said.

As the ceiling parted above us, I was asking myself the same question. Then the floor began to rise.

CHAPTER 25

DEATH MATCH

The bloodthirsty cheering grew louder as the floor lifted us into view.

Grandma stared down at Kayla.

"Tell me you have something, girl," she said.

"I think we can buy a little time," said Kayla. "If you and Happy work together."

Grandma looked toward Dad.

"No," said Kayla. "You and Happy *Junior.* Remember the partnership you were planning? The present you were going to give him in the solarium? It's still in your pocket."

"Yeah," I said. "The present! What was the present?"

The floor stopped. We stood in a corner of an enormous wrestling ring, surrounded by thousands of screaming aliens.

"The offer's been revoked," said Grandma. "He threw it back in my face. That partnership is off the table."

"Well, you'd better put it back on the table," said Kayla, "if you want to survive the next ten seconds."

In the far corner of the ring, Florida Pete—his face bloody from raw meat—had risen up on his own platform. He thrashed furiously against his chains. The foam around his mouth turned pink as it mixed with the blood. It was quite a sight.

"Grandma," said Kayla, pointing at Grandma's pocket. "The partnership. Reoffer it. Now."

"Must I?" said Grandma.

"You must," said Kayla.

Grandma extended her open hand toward me.

"Shake her hand, Happy," said Kayla.

Shrugging, I shook Grandma's hand.

"Good," said Kayla. "You're officially partners. Try to lure Pete over toward the ropes."

"Very well," said Grandma, taking the little black present from her pocket. "This way, Happy Junior."

As I followed Grandma toward the center of the ring, I watched Florida Pete howl and thrash against his chains. Grandma handed me the little gift. I popped it open and removed a disk of spangled black-and-red fabric.

"What kind of partnership is this?" I asked.

"Tag team," said Grandma. "Put it on."

In my hands was a black wrestling mask emblazoned with spangled red roses. I looked toward Grandma and saw that she was fitting an identical mask over her own face, with her long, elegant, and *familiar* fingers.

It finally clicked.

"Grandma," I said. "You're the Masked Flamenco!"

"*We* are the Masked Flamencos, partner," she said. "Now put your face on. And tuck in that ridiculous beard!"

I shoved my beard down into my undershirt and put the mask over my face.

As soon as it was down around my ears, I realized that mask was no ordinary piece of fabric, but something high-tech that Dad must have built. I heard faint but irresistible Spanish guitar music. My body could not help moving and flowing to the sound. My fists went to my hips. My right foot stomped. I reached up and clapped twice. Grandma did the same, in perfect unison. Entwining our arms, we began a flamenco stride toward the center of the ring.

This sight made Pete howl and thrash even more violently.

A bell dinged. Pete's chains fell to the floor. He charged us like a mad rhino.

Grandma twirled me around several times and sent me spinning off toward him like a top. Inspired rather than controlled by the music, I executed a balletic leap, six feet into the air, and slapped Pete twice across the face. *Slap-slap*. Flipping over his head, I landed on my toes, with a stylish arm flourish.

The crowd roared. Pete howled and reeled around at me. I danced away, keeping barely inches in front of his clawing grasp. He would have caught and killed me for sure if Grandma hadn't leapt in, tagged my hand, and pirouetted both her boots across Pete's face. Then he chased after Grandma until I danced in and tagged her reaching hand. By repeating variations of this tag-team strategy, we maneuvered Pete across the ring and up to the side ropes.

As I dove over the top ropes, Pete lunged for me, then got himself hooked around backward as I danced back under the bottom ropes.

The moment Pete became tangled, Kayla leapt into view with something silver shining in her hands: Frank Segar's handcuffs. She hooked one end around Pete's wrist, the other around his boot. Not only was Pete caught, he was bent over backward in a sort of pretzel shape.

Now my mom, dad, and sisters leapt into the mix, trying to wrestle Pete down into submission.

"Wait!" Kayla yelled above the melee. "Grandma, make him recognize you."

Lifting her mask, Grandma stooped down toward Pete. "It's me, Pete!" she yelled. "It's the boss lady! Remember, Pete?"

Pete's foam-drenched face grimaced up at her, his eyes rolling around wildly. She held out her hand, and Pete sniffed it skeptically.

"Boss . . . lady?" said Pete, sniffing.

"Yes, Pete," said Grandma.

"Did I win, Boss? Do I get my *re*ward?"

"Yes," said Grandma. "But you need to stop fighting. Don't fight anymore, and you'll get your *re*ward."

"You're always changing the rules!" said Pete. "I want my Specs! I want my *re*ward now!"

"Here, take them," said Beth, handing Pete her Specs. "These are your Specs now. Take them."

This could not have been easy for Beth, and we all appreciated it, especially Pete. A look of blissful relief spread over his face as he finally held the Specs in his own hand. His eyes brimmed over with tears, and he began to cry and laugh at the same time.

"I'll never have to hurt another soul," said Pete. And he pulled us all into a big one-armed bear hug. Then we all began to hug each other and laugh with pure relief that the fight was finally over. As we did so, a strange buzzing sound began to come from the audience.

"What's that?" I asked Kayla.

"They're booing," she said.

This brought a big fat grin to my face. I whooped with delight. Their disappointment over us not dying made me so happy that I marched out into the ring holding my arms up in triumph.

The alien booing grew louder.

"Really, Hap," said Grandma, walking up beside me. "If you must play the heel, at least do it properly."

Smiling, Grandma wheeled her arm around in several circles and brought her cupped hand to her ear, as though the booing was the sweetest sound she had ever heard and she couldn't get enough. The crowd *really* hated this. So I began doing it too. Soon the boos became screams of thunderous anger. It felt great.

"Uh, guys?" said Kayla.

"Not now, Kayla," said Grandma, thumbing her nose

at the audience while I shook my butt at them. "We're having a moment."

Mom joined our antics out there and began gesturing and swearing at the aliens in Romanian. I had never heard such bad language, let alone from Mom. It infuriated the aliens, who now began throwing their drinking vessels and half-eaten panini at us.

"Guys!" yelled Kayla. "Guys! Get back here now! They're about to cut the artificial gravity! Grab the ropes! Everybody grab the ropes!"

We made it back just in time to grab hold of the ropes before they cut the gravity, and we all began to float.

"Who's doing this?" yelled Dad.

"The Gubbinses," said Kayla. "This crowd wants a death match. And they're going to have a riot if they don't get one. So they're unleashing the champion."

"Oh no," I said. "Not the spiked eel thing."

But I was already watching the enormous liquid-like monster flow into the arena.

The crowd raged with bloodthirsty delight.

The horrid spiked eel twirled and climbed through the air like a roller coaster. It shot straight up toward the rafters. Then, baring its long rows of fangs, it plunged straight down toward us.

"Unlock the bracelets," said Florida Pete. "I got this feller."

Kayla quickly picked the lock on the handcuffs using

the same hairpin from earlier. With lightning speed, Pete pulled himself hand-over-hand to the ropes across the corner from us. Then squatting down, he compressed his body into a ball beneath the lowest rope. He stared up into the monster's approaching fangs.

"Come'n git it, Jabroni," said Pete.

Then he yanked down the top rope, stepped onto it, and, like an arrow from a bow, launched himself straight upward.

The spiked eel monster had a moment to look surprised before Pete caught it with a hard uppercut to the chin.

"Whooo-ooop!" whooped Pete. He ran sideways across the beast's fangs. He plunged one fist into its nostril and began punching it in the eye with his other.

Howling, the spiked eel reeled wildly off into space.

As I stared up at this in amazement, I noticed something interesting float by closer down to the ring: a panini. This, in and of itself, wasn't unusual. The air was crowded with panini. But this one in particular caught my eye, because it had two little lizard legs kicking out from one end. The webbed feet of the lizard propelled the pressed sandwich along like a kickboard through a swimming pool.

"It's Squeep!" I yelled. Climbing up, I hooked my shoe under the top rope and reached high up into the air. But the lizard-panini was still several yards beyond my grasping fingers.

"Dad!" I yelled. "Help me get higher!"

My dad grabbed me by the ankles and lifted me higher. Then my mom grabbed him around the ankles, and we formed an extending and weightless human ladder, until I could yank the panini out of the air.

I tried to pull Squeep! out of the pressed sandwich, like a cork from a bottle, but the top half of his body was caught on something. I began ripping away at the bready exterior and the lettuce until I saw Squeep!'s big yellow eyes blinking at me. He clutched in his webbed fingers a disk covered in chipotle mayo. At first I thought it was a tomato slice. But when I wiped away the pink goop, I saw silver underneath. Squeep! had brought us the makeup compact! I couldn't believe the ingenuity of this lizard! I hugged him ecstatically, and he licked my face in return.

I yelled down to my dad, who still gripped me around the ankles. "It's the compact! Pass it down to Alice!"

I handed it down to Dad, who handed it down to Mom, who handed it to Alice. I had never seen her happier. She shook the goop off its exterior, readying to pop it open.

"Okay!" yelled Alice. "Everyone hold hands! We all have to be touching for me to pull us in!"

I looked above me.

"Wait!" I yelled down at her. "We can't leave Florida Pete here! We need to get Pete!"

The world champion was focused on his fight with the galactic champion. But on a close pass he heard me screaming his name. Glancing over, he saw me splayed out in midair waving a lizard at him. He nodded at me like a passing fighter pilot in combat.

Then Pete plunged both his boots hard into the eel beast's eye and kicked off into a backward dive down toward the ring. His form was perfect until, at the last moment, the whipping tail of the eel cracked into the side of his head, knocking him unconscious and onto a different trajectory altogether. My heart sank. Now I wouldn't be able to reach him.

"Get me higher!" I yelled down at my family.

Eliza grabbed hold of my mom's ankles. Beth grabbed hold of Eliza's ankles. Kayla grabbed Beth's, Alice grabbed Kayla's, and Grandma grabbed Alice's, until our human chain extended me far enough out into space for me to grab Pete's big red wrestling boot.

But no sooner had I secured Pete than I heard my mom scream down below me. Then everyone started to scream. Looking down, I saw what had happened. In all the excitement, Baby Lu had squirmed free of whoever had been holding her and was now floating into space.

"Grab her!" they were all yelling. "Grab the baby!"

Baby Lu floated up toward me like a little golden soap bubble. I thought I could just about reach out and grab her, if I let go of Pete, or if I let go of Squeep! Who should it be? As I wondered, an enormous fanged face swam into view behind Baby Lu. The spiked monster was rushing straight toward us, jaws opening.

Let go of Pete, I told myself.

I rethought, just as quickly, *No. He's a person. I can't just . . .*

But then I had an idea. I began nodding my head up and down as hard as I could, hitching the entire length of my beard out of my undershirt.

Then I flung the beard out as far as I could toward Baby Lu.

"Grab hold!" I yelled.

Reaching out with both her little fists, Baby Lu clutched hold of it. What an amazing little kid!

"Got her!" I yelled down. "Alice, take us home!"

"Alice, take us home!" yelled Dad. "Alice, take us home!" yelled Mom. And so on . . . As the statement echoed down my family, I watched the fangs of the eel encircle us.

As they snapped down, we vanished from that world.

CHAPTER 26

THE RETURN

The entire family, plus a lizard and a wrestler, tumbled in a pile onto the cedar-planked floor of the Doorganizer.

Rolling to my feet, I looked around to make sure everyone was still there. But where was Baby Lu?

"Baby Lu!" I yelled.

"Shh. I've got her," said Grandma, who stood cradling Baby Lu in her arms.

"Oh, thank God," I said. "Here, you can give her to me now."

"You still don't trust me, Happy?" said Grandma. "After I just saved her life?"

"*I* just saved her life," I said. "With my beard."

"If it weren't for me, you wouldn't even have that beard," said Grandma.

"Quiet, everyone," said Dad. "We need to get out of the Doorganizer before it becomes catastrophic. This is extra-dimensional space. We can't be in here. Especially Kayla! Kayla, honey, close your eyes."

"I feel fine," said Kayla, but she closed them.

"Alice," said Dad. "Can you get us out?"

"I don't know," said Alice. "Hap opened the last portal to Earth. Where's the portal, Hap?"

"Uh," I said, looking around at the mess. "Squeep! knows the way out. Where is he?"

"Is that this sweet little bugger's name?" said Florida Pete, who sat cradling Squeep! in his tree-trunk-size arms. "He's a beauty, all right. I bet he's never hurt a soul. Maybe I won't be a turtle, maybe I'll be a Squeep! What's his natural habitat?"

"An elementary school," I said.

"Perfect," said Pete. "Play with the kids, teach them about science, and never hurt a soul."

"He eats bugs," I said.

"Do they have souls?" asked Pete.

"I don't know," I said. "Do sponges?"

"Good point," said Pete. "I'm gonna do it now. I can't risk ever becoming violent again."

"Uh," said Dad. "We need to get Kayla out of here. We need to get her out *now*."

But Florida Pete couldn't wait. He put on the glasses, looked at Squeep!, and flicked the switch.

Now we had two lizards instead of one. Knowing firsthand how hard new bodies can be to acclimate to,

204

I decided to carry Pete the lizard in my pocket so he wouldn't get lost.

As Squeep! led us through the wending pathways of Alice's stolen stuff, Dad kept his hand clamped over Kayla's eyes. I wondered why he was so worried about her in here. What was the mysterious conflict between Kayla's powers and the Doorganizer's? I knew she had never been able to see into it or predict what happened inside . . .

Before I had much time to ponder this, good old Squeep! had returned us to the little shell-shaped mirror on the floor. It was right where I had left it, just past my old library books. We linked hands, and Alice brought us through the portal and back into our bedroom.

As before, it was a great relief to get out of the Doorganizer.

But the relief was short-lived.

The first thing we noticed once we stood safely back in the bedroom was about a dozen FBI agents surrounding us with their weapons drawn.

"Get on your knees and put your hands behind your head!" said a familiar voice.

Looking up, I saw Detective Frank Segar. I had left the portal open, and I was happy that Frank had found his way out. I smiled at him. He did not smile back.

"I said get on your knees and put your hands behind your head," said Frank.

They cuffed Alice first, then Grandma, then Dad. I guess they figured the rest of us weren't dangerous.

As the FBI agents led Grandma away, she turned, looked back at me, and smiled.

"Tag you soon, partner," she said.

CHAPTER 27

LINGERING SIDE EFFECTS

ROSS — POLICE LINE- DO NOT CROSS

First, they made Dad shut down and destroy all the technology that could lead the aliens into our world or us into theirs. Dad was only too happy to do so. It meant separating Alice from her Doorganizer. The Gubbinses had given him an idea of how this might be possible. But it had to be done immediately, before anything else could be taken out of the compact. So if Alice ever stole anything from you, sorry, you won't be getting it back.

Then the US government seized control of Conklin Industries, Conklin Manor, and all of my family's assets. And they took us into custody.

"So after all that," I said to Kayla, "we're just going to end up in the Last Hexagon anyway?"

"Not really," she said. "In this hexagon, the family gets to stay together."

"How?" I said. "What's different now?"

"Grandma," she said.

"Because she got caught too?" I said.

"Partly," said Kayla. "But also going through all that with us changed her. She's adjusting her plans now."

"Ha!" I said. "She'll never change."

But then, to my surprise, Grandma not only pled guilty, she took the rap for all the illegal activity. She blamed herself not only for Dad's involvement, but for all of Alice's thievery as well.

Did I truly think Grandma's heart had melted, and she had suddenly become a good person? No. I'm not stupid. I thought, *What's she up to now?*

In exchange for cooperating with government scientists, Dad only got probation. And Mom could stay in the country. Alice got a week in juvenile detention and a state-appointed psychiatrist named Dr. Jeremy. All in all, the only person besides Grandma to see any jail time was Mr. Abernathy, the zookeeper.

I finally got to return Squeep! to my school, along with a new, identical lizard named Pete, who wore funny little green glasses and had a mustache. All the kids loved Pete the lizard, and he loved them. He also loved his little terrarium. Unfortunately, I can't say the same for Squeep!, who had caught the taste for adventure. All that time inside the Doorganizer had taught him skills no lizard should know. These days, he's always escaping from the terrarium, the classroom, and the school. Most mornings I wake up to find that he has snuck back into my room and is curled up on my chest asleep.

We have an apartment now near the hotel where Mom works. It's small by most standards, but luxurious compared to Grandma's basement. I even have my own room—that is, if you don't count the Squeepmeister.

Eliza hates that she still has to share a room, though now it's only with Beth.

"I should have my own palace!" says Eliza.

During their time together, Grandma filled Eliza's head with a lot of nonsense about how someday our family would take over the whole galaxy, and that we would all become kings and queens, each running our own solar system from our own palace planets. Sometimes I worry that Eliza has actually bought into Grandma's bundle of baloney.

The FBI "requested" that Dad take a little break from inventing. Mostly, he's complying, though he has been working on a new medicine for Beth, who developed a lingering side effect from wearing the Perfect-O-Specs for so many years.

One morning Beth woke up from a strange dream to find that she looked just like Eliza again. It wore off after a few hours. But then, a week later, Beth woke up from an even stranger dream to find herself looking like a totally different girl that none of us recognized. This wore off too, though while it lasted Beth could only speak Portuguese. My dad created a drink for Beth to take before she goes to bed. He also taught Beth a self-hypnosis technique to prevent her from dreaming that she's anyone other than herself. He says that should resolve the issue.

Kayla is still good friends with Alphonso, though she tries not to bother him with too many questions these days, which has made her life a lot more enjoyable.

And I guess you've probably read about the rest of the story online or in the newspapers.

Personally, I can't say that I was surprised by the news that Grandma had vanished from her prison cell without a trace. I know there's a nationwide manhunt, but I don't think they'll ever find her. At least not on this planet.

I admit, the thought of Grandma at large in the universe makes me uneasy. Especially when I think of the last thing she said to me.

What on earth had she meant by that?

Tag you soon, partner.

Not too soon, I hope.